Saved Race

STEPHANIE PERRY MOORE

The Negro National Anthem

Lift every voice and sing
Till earth and heaven ring,
Ring with the harmonies of Liberty;
Let our rejoicing rise
High as the listening skies,
Let it resound loud as the rolling sea.
Sing a song full of the faith that the dark past has taught us,
Sing a song full of the hope that the present has brought us,
Facing the rising sun of our new day begun
Let us march on till victory is won.

So begins the Black National Anthem, by James Weldon Johnson in 1900. Lift Every Voice is the name of the joint imprint of The Institute for Black Family Development and Moody Press, a division of the Moody Bible Institute.

Our vision is to advance the cause of Christ through publishing African-American Christians who educate, edify, and disciple Christians in the church community through quality books written for African Americans.

The Institute for Black Family Development is a national Christian organization. It offers degreed and nondegreed training nationally and internationally to established and emerging leaders from churches and Christian organizations. To learn more about The Institute for Black Family Development write us at:

The Institute for Black Family Development
15151 Faust
Detroit, Michigan 48223

Moody Press, a ministry of Moody Bible Institute,
is designed for education, evangelization, and edification.
If we may assist you in knowing more about Christ
and the Christian life, please write us without obligation:

Moody Press
c/o Moody Literature Ministries
820 N. LaSalle Blvd.
Chicago, Illinois 60610.

Saved Race

STEPHANIE PERRY MOORE

Moody Press   "Lift Every Voice"

Edited by Diane Reeder
Cover Illustration by Tito Cuenca
Cover Design by Keith Senator

ISBN: 0-8024-4238-2

1 3 5 7 9 10 8 6 4 2
Printed in the United States of America

*For three biracial women from different generations
who have a special place in my heart:*

My maternal grandmother - Mrs. Viola Roundtree

My dear girlfriend - Mrs. Sarah Hunter

My goddaughter - Lil' Miss Danielle Lynn

*May the world learn that in the end the only race that is
going to count is the one that is saved!*

Contents

Acknowledgments

As I color with my girls using the eight crayons in the Crayola box, I'm in awe at the final picture that splashes the colors together. Then I reflect on my writing and the color of several important people that help make me the best author I can be. Thanks to all who continue to help me learn that nothing is more important than saving souls for Christ.

To my reading pool, Sierra Hunter, Kimmie Johnson, Cyndi Lynn, Cole Smith, and Trace Williams, and my assistant, Tiffany Austin: You all color my writing **ORANGE**. Orange is such a bright color and that is what each of you give me . . . bright ideas. I am grateful to you for making time to read and edit my rough work. Your input has saved this novel from being less than what God wanted it to be.

To everyone at Moody Press, especially Cynthia Ballenger: You all are the color **GREEN**. When I think of green I think of growth. I am grateful to you for your financial investment and belief in the Payton Skky series. Your resources have saved this project from never being placed on the shelves and never blessing a soul.

To my parents, Franklin and Shirley Perry and my brother, Dennis: You all color me with **BROWN**. The brown comes from the strong roots into which I was born. I thank you for serving me with your love all of my life. Your support has saved me many times from the failure of "not trying."

To my daughters, Sydni and Sheldyn: You two precious girls color me **PURPLE**. All I have to say is Barney, and we have a great time. I am grateful that you both motivate me daily to be that best mom, person, and writer that I can be. Your dependence has saved me from complacency.

To the gals I discipled, Jocelyn Bush, Shana Ogelsby, and Antisha Oates: You all color me with **YELLOW**. Three

Spelman young ladies that are bright, sweet, and warm-hearted. I am grateful that you trusted me with your spiritual growth this year. Your passion to know Christ saved me from not growing as a Christian myself.

To the reader, staring at this page: You color me with **BLACK**. The ink on the bare page was written to inspire you to love God more. I am grateful that of all the things you could be doing, you have taken the time to read *Saved Race*. Your need to be both challenged and entertained has saved me from not writing this book.

To my husband, Derrick Moore: You color me with **RED**. My heart is filled with love because of how you make me feel. I am grateful for all you do for our family, which affords me the opportunity to write. Your headship has saved me time and time again from going against God's will for my life.

And to Jesus Christ: You color me with **WHITE**! Because of You I can be pure. I am grateful that You have deemed me worthy to write Christian stories. Your call on my life has saved me from doing worldly things! I pray everyone learns and lives Your will for their lives!

Finishing the Statement

W e know the color of our skin, yet when we go out into the world, we do not need to be afraid to feel like we're equal to anyone else. In Christ we are excellent, and we can compete with the very best," I voiced with pride to my brown classmates.

Although that sounded arrogant, I knew it was true. We all fall short of excellence, but God is perfect. Thanks to His presence in a sinful me, I can claim His goodness.

Continuing, I encouraged, "And because of His love for us, we can be all that anyone else can be. And don't misunderstand: I'm not even saying we're better because we're black; I'm saying because we're saved, because Jesus' blood is running through us, we can overcome any obstacle that is before us. We can climb over mountains that will be hard to climb, and we can get through valleys that are deep and depressing, and we can achieve. Just remember to seek ye first, and my prayer, as I close, is that all of your dreams will be given. Thanks."

It was weird receiving a standing ovation, especially when I didn't even know that Pastor McClep was going to put me on the spot. He had asked me to stand before my graduating class and give a baccalaureate speech. I didn't know what I was going to say but it just came. It came naturally. Our past. Our present. Our future. Words of wisdom from God flowed to my lips, to say to my friends that we are to be congratulated. And as they saluted me, I humbly accepted the praise, and applauded them in return.

"Let's give her another round of applause," my pastor said as I was taking my seat. "We're really proud of you, Payton, really proud of you."

Humbly I smiled. "Thank you, Sir."

At that moment, I felt loved by my parents, my peers, and even myself. I was proud of me, and I so hoped God was as well. I had a lot to learn, but I was working towards it. And although I had failed in several areas in my life, like being angry at God and choosing lust over the love of Christ, I hoped I had become a stronger person for my mistakes.

After the service, I went down to the reception hall, and was greeted first by Tad Taylor, a guy who I wasn't even sure was my boyfriend or my good friend. Either way, I had serious feelings for him that ran deep as the ocean's bottom. He reached over and planted a sweet peck on my cheek.

"We're proud of you, lady. That was an awesome speech. You want some punch?"

"Yeah, that would be great," I told him.

"Cool . . . I'll be right back."

"So, what's up? You gon' be a motivational speaker or something?" my girlfriend Dymond joked.

It was so good to be with my friends. I hugged Dymond Johnson, Rain Crandle, and Lynzi Brown really tight, for in the back of my mind, I knew that pretty soon the four of us wouldn't be together. We would go on from this place and hear our names called in a couple days, get our diplomas, spend our summers in different places, and hopefully come back together once more to get ready for school and depart for different destinations. At least Lynzi and I would be off to the same university.

I just hoped our future would never take us to places where we'd be marrying men with different interests, living in cities far away, and having careers that wouldn't allow reunions. All of that would hinder us from being close like this again. However, I couldn't and didn't know the future, so I held on extra tight, and in my mind thanked God for friends like these in high school. The past four years with them had been a blast.

"Oooh, yo' church got a spread," Lynzi said, cracking a smile.

"Well, I see the patient has gotten better."

"Yeah, I'm still a little weak. I can't stand up too long, but I can definitely say I'm on the right track."

This was a day of blessings. My crazy friend, Lynzi, had had a horrible car accident just a few short weeks ago. No one thought she would survive that ordeal. The God I know and love is truly a miracle worker. As I stood there and looked at the miracle before me, I came to understand God even better.

Mr. and Mrs. Perry Skky Sr., my parents, started walking toward my girlfriends and me. The smile on their faces made me feel good inside.

My dad is a successful automobile dealer and my mom is a "domestic engineer." Though she stays at home, she is very active in the community. It is her forte. She is a success in her own right, raising lots of money for several causes that wouldn't have made it without her. She always makes sure to give God the credit, though. I knew my parents were proud of me. Mom's humility and my dad's business sense are what make me proud of them. Seeing their eyes shine with accomplishment for who I had become made me feel good all over.

My dad reached out and gave me a hug. My mom kept smiling. Although they didn't tell me, for once in my life I knew I had done OK. Where I would go from here was uncertain. Where I had been to get to this point was quite crazy, especially this last year. But for one shining moment, I was glad they were glad that I had done OK.

"You'd better c'mon," my brother, Perry, said to me in haste later that afternoon. "Yo' boys about to fight."

I had no clue what he was talking about. Perry had been known to exaggerate, but this time his actions of haste seemed as if something was up. I followed him to the church parking lot, where I saw Tad and Dakari, my ex-boyfriend, all up in each other's faces.

"Oh no, see, we're not having this," I stepped in between them and said. "We're on church grounds and y'all acting like y'all in the streets somewhere. I'm not gon' have my parents, my pastor, or anybody come out here and see y'all actin' crazy. Don't trip!"

"You think I was about to fight him?" Tad said.

"I don't know what's going on. All I know is that y'all are getting loud; my brother comes to get me, and y'all confronting each other and stuff. I mean, what else am I suppose to think? The two of you are best friends? Tuh, I don't think so! It's obvious y'all can't even be in the same room. At least be cordial enough to enjoy the same air. What is this about?"

"Man . . . it ain't nothin' . . . it ain't nothin'," Dakari said.

"Yeah, you right, it's nothin'." Tad attacked verbally. "You step to me like that again, we gon' have some problems. That's all I have to say."

Both of them were tight-lipped about what it was that had the two of them upset. It kinda bothered me. I really wondered what was up. Tad came over and kissed me on the cheek, sorta abruptly, and said he'd call me later. Then Tad disappeared. Dakari simply left the scene without even saying good-bye.

As I watched the cute guy of my past walk away, our history came to mind. He had been the one that held my heart for most of my high school days. However, in the beginning of our senior year, he decided since I wasn't putting out, he wasn't going to put up with me. He dissed me for another girl. A girl who started meeting some of his physical needs. I am grateful he broke up with me because I kept my virginity. Also, I found and fell for a wonderful guy, Tad Taylor. However, seeing my ex get in his car, seeing Dakari Ross Graham driving away . . . I knew the connection was still there.

"Girl, you better get over that," Lynzi came up behind me and exclaimed.

"See, why you all up in my business? This ain't about you."

"Well, it don't need to be about Dakari. For real. For real."

"I don't know, Lynzi. I don't think it's about Dakari. I just think that for some reason he still means something."

"But what about Tad?" she questioned.

That was a good question. What about Tad? I had to truly ask myself. What was up? If I cared about Tad, why would Dakari even still be an issue? Why all the guy drama anyway? I should be focused on what's about to come in my life, but when I thought about college, I couldn't get rid of the two of them, because the three of us were all going to the same college, the University of Georgia.

"You gon' have a lot of trouble next year at school," Lynzi said, reading my mind.

"Yeah, you're right, but at least I'll have you there."

"Um, that's kinda what I wanted to talk to you about. Girl, I'm joining the army. I just need some discipline in my life. I need some structure. I'm not ready for college yet. I don't even know what it is I wanna be."

I couldn't say anything. A part of my heart just sank. Not going to school with Lynzi! She was my girl. I was counting on her to be my roommate at Georgia. Lynzi not going? I couldn't comprehend the thought.

"Ahhh, don't even act like that," she said after seeing the dejection on my face. "You'll be fine."

Since I exempted my exams, I was helping my teacher, Mrs. Guice, take down some of the boards in her room—trying to make graduation come faster, I guess. Though I should have been relaxing, my mind was weighed down with many different things: college, guys, and expectations. I was so burdened with stuff.

My thoughts were interrupted when the frail Caucasian woman in her midfifties called out to me. "Payton, hon, as I sit here looking at you, you pretty thing, I'm just at a loss for words." It was funny seeing her all emotional. Although she was tiny, she was a powerful lady. She kept all of us on our p's and q's. I had never seen this side of Mrs. Guice, and I didn't know how to respond, so I just sat there, waiting for her to open up.

After taking a deep breath, she said, "When I came to this school fifteen years ago, I had apprehensions. You know, me being a young white lady teaching at a school that was predominantly black was very tough on me, but I overcame that and learned we are all the same. You opened my eyes. I really never met an African-American young lady who had as much poise and class and style as you."

15

Mrs. Guice was silent after saying all that. I guess she was waiting on a response from me. My teacher was just staring.

At first I was a little hesitant. Kinda rubbed me the wrong way. I had just completed a debutante ball, where there were fifty girls who had poise and style and were "all that." Not because we were African-American women, but just because. Still, I was able to accept her comment in the way that it was meant—as a compliment and not a critique. However, I still didn't know what to say. I, too, was at a loss for words. I just smiled and took it in.

When the bell rang for school to be over, I headed out the door on my way home. I was planning on going to the senior movie night. First I needed to change clothes, get a bite to eat, and pick up my girls. Before I got to my jeep, Dakari pulled up in front of me in a fly, red hot Ferrari.

"Please get in. We really need to talk," he pleaded.

I was hesitant and didn't move. He stopped his brother's car in the middle of the street. He got out. He came around. He opened the other door and practically put me in the new car.

"You got some nerve," I told him when he started driving me away.

"I apologize for being so abrupt, but we need to settle some things. I just wanted to talk to you and let you know what was really going on. I needed to tell you what was up before yo' boy got to you, and you know . . . just messed up your mind. I wanted you to hear from me what was up."

"What are you talking about?" I uttered, in a state of confusion.

"I'm talking about what we were discussing yesterday at your church. Um, I just wanna tell you what we were talking about because I think you should hear it from me. It might sound offensive if it comes from anyone else. And that's not the way it is intended. I care . . . I really care about you, and I don't want to throw away whatever it is we got 'cause somebody tells you something I said and misrepresents me."

I leaned back against the car door. My seat belt was still on, but yet, I was turned, and I was just checking the brother out. He was trippin'. He was really worrying about something that didn't seem so serious to me. Tad hadn't even called me last night, so obviously it wasn't that big a deal, or was it? Did Dakari upset Tad so much that he couldn't even call?

"You better slow down. You're going mighty fast," I said to Dakari as we drove through historic Augusta.

"I got this; just listen because this is major. Basically, I just told the guy that he might say he's all holy roly and everything, and that the sex stuff might not be an issue, but, um, the more he hangs around you . . . I mean, I'm a man . . . I know it's gon' be an issue, and I told him he better not compromise you in any way. 'Cause if there's any disrespecting going on, then it's gon' be me and him."

I was digesting the information and Dakari was still speeding. Before anything could be uttered or exchanged between the two of us, lights started flashing from behind. We got pulled over by a cop who wasn't too friendly. The guy had Dakari outside the car with his hands on top of the hood. Yes, Dakari was speeding, but all the roughness and the hard-core treatment, I felt, was way too premature. Especially since Dakari was extremely respectful to the officer.

I couldn't help but feel that this was one of those race incidents because the cop was white and Dakari was black. Driving While Black is a serious issue. I just never experienced it until now. And I felt that moment was D. W. B. because of the circumstances and negative vibes we were getting from the cop. Not because I feel all cops are racist, but because this one had no regard for my friend's welfare.

The cop confirmed it when he ignorantly uttered out of

17

his mouth: "You people do this all the time. Thinking you can get away with this or that. I don't know; y'all are always carrying weapons, I have to protect myself. Get out the car, and don't say one word, 'cause if you do, then you'll be in jail like the rest of your . . . what do y'all call it? Brothas and sistahs."

I knew Dakari wanted to go off. I knew he wanted to say so many things. So did I, but I was scared. The cop was an authority and even though he was wrong, he had the upper hand. I just kept praying quietly to myself. So many times over the last couple of days, I wanted to say something but didn't know quite what to say. I told Dakari to keep his mouth shut. Sometimes words aren't necessary. You just have to pray and let God handle it. Sometimes you don't have to have the answers. Sometimes you can't say what you really feel. You just have to let the Holy Spirit take control. At that horrific moment when so much of me was dying to come out, I realized that in life you won't always be finishing the statement.

2

Calling
My Name

ayton . . . PAYTON, call my brother! He's at my house,"
Dakari yelled as the cop jerked both his hands behind
him.

"What did you do, young man, steal this car?" Officer
Briggs interrogated. "There's no tag on the back. You can't
find any registration for me. Where'd you get it from? Is the
young lady involved? I know it's not yours; you're too
young to have a job."

"Oh, my gosh . . . oh, my gosh. What's his number?
What's his number?" I said in a state of panic.

I was watching the cop harass my friend. I couldn't even
remember Dakari's number, which, back in the day, I used
to dial all the time. All of a sudden Dakari's pager went off.
I decided to dial the number that came up on the screen. I
remembered Dakari saying he had to meet back up with his
brother to switch cars. Logic and hope told me it just had to
be Drake. So I called the number.

"Man, give me my ride," Drake yelled into the receiver thinking it was Dakari.

"No, no Drake, this is Payton. Payton Skky, your brother's friend."

"Payton? Heeyyy, little lady, what's up? He told me that you overheard our conversation that night. I want to apol . . . "

"No. No. No. We don't have time for all that." I cut him off and said, "Dakari's in trouble. He's really in big trouble."

I gave him the directions and told him to get to us quickly. I told him that if he didn't get there soon, both Dakari and I might be behind bars. That's just how crazy this cop seemed to me. When I got off the phone, Dakari's left cheek was smeared into the shiny red hood. Both hands were clasped tightly behind his head.

"Lord," I prayed, "I know every person in the world isn't prejudiced, but I do know this cop that's with Dakari now ain't on the up-and-up. You know what I'm saying. Help us before he hurts us. Hear this prayer, Lord. Please, hear this prayer."

No sooner than I finished praying did Drake pull up in Dakari's ride, an old Corvette. Treasured by many but it was in a whole different league from the Ferrari we were in.

"Watch your back back now, son," the gut-bulging, red-cheeked man said to Drake.

"Oh, sir, I don't want no trouble," Drake attested, throwing his hands up in the air. "My name is Drake Graham, just graduated from the University of Georgia. I'm on my way to go to the Falcons' training camp in a couple of months. Just signed an NFL contract. No trouble, sir. No trouble from me."

"Drake Graham! You're Drake Graham," the cop totally changed his voice and said. "I'm a big Bull Dawg fan. Went to Georgia. Kids went to Georgia. I've been watching you all year. Linebacker. Dang, you can hit."

"So what's the trouble, Officer? Can you let my lil' brother up?" Drake asked with total composure, as if the cop were a friend.

"Your brother? This is your brother? Ohhh, OK . . . OK," the cop said as he lifted his hand from Dakari's face and dusted off his back.

There was no relief in my ex-boyfriend's eyes. They were bloodshot red. Only rage and hate. Though it wasn't olden times, like the times my great-great-grandmother talked about, working for the "massa," it sure felt like it. Drake smoothed everything over, and the cop apologized time and time again. It wasn't enough for me, and I could tell it surely wasn't enough for Dakari, but Drake felt it was best to leave the situation alone. *Where's the justice in that?* I thought.

Yes, I understood that every cop wasn't this way, but for the ones that are, how are we ever going to get rid of them? How are we going to challenge them to uphold the law and treat everyone equally? If we don't prosecute and don't stand up for what's right, they get away with stuff like this. And the next brotha might not have an NFL brotha. The next brotha pulled over because of D.W. B. might be found D.O.A. But it wasn't my call to make. So, we switched cars with Drake, and Dakari took me home.

"Dakari . . . Dakari, talk to me." I tried to get him to open up.

He was so upset, so frustrated he couldn't even speak. His growing manhood was shattered. I could only hope, as I watched tears drip from his face like a running faucet, that he'd be able to shake this thing and get back to normal.

The next day was the day I'd waited for since kindergarten. I was a graduate. I was about to accomplish something great. I was about to get papers that would tell me I could move on. We were supposed to wear white dresses under our caps and gowns. However, no one really seemed to care. Jeans and white T-shirts are what we all agreed as a class to wear. And, although it was silly, I just had to participate. One more fun thing for the road.

I had never worn jeans and pumps before. White pumps at that. It wasn't a cute outfit, but it was cute that we all did it. Trust me, it was a fashion fad that would fade real fast—like right after graduation.

When I was on the coliseum floor, I looked up to find my family. When I spotted them, I was surprised to see so many of my kinfolk: aunts, uncles, cousins. I was especially surprised to see my first cousin, Pillar. Seeing her was a little much. I never expected to see her at my graduation. Pillar and I didn't have much of a relationship.

If I remember correctly, Pillar had just gotten out of school. For her to get out of school and come all the way from Denver for me just seemed a little much to believe. But, nonetheless, there she was in the stands. Maybe our last visit, since it was pleasant, erased all those years of distance. Maybe the two of us could be friends, after all. We couldn't do anything about being family, but we were always able to avoid being friends. Maybe now that would change.

With Dymond being our valedictorian and all, I was saddened to see her face before the ceremony. She wasn't happy at first and none of us knew why. Then I remembered. When we were all standing outside to line up, Fatz had been nowhere to be found.

Finally Lynzi asked Dymond, "Where is Fatz? He's going to miss walking in."

She said with exhaustion and depression, "He's not gonna be able to graduate right now. He failed some class, and he's gotta take it this summer, and they won't let him walk."

"Are you serious?" I probed.

Rain interjected, "That's awful, girl."

"See . . . now they know they could have let that boy walk," Lynzi said powerfully.

"It's a lot of people missing," Dy informed us.

Actually, it was quite sad. And not just his situation. Dymond was correct that the majority of our senior class wasn't walking for one reason or another. Out of three hundred and something kids, we only had a little over a hundred walking. Administration didn't do their job. Parents didn't do their job. Seniors surely didn't do their job . . . well, maybe the buck should stop with me. Not that I'm sooo smart, but surely instead of all the parties we had throughout the year, I should have been encouraging my buddies to get in their books. But I didn't know. Everybody procrastinates. Sooner or later what's done in the dark comes to light.

Dymond explained that at least there was a good side to Fatz's situation. With summer school he'd go on to college next year. But most people who weren't going to be graduating were going to have to repeat the twelfth grade. That wasn't good. Four years of high school was enough. Who'd want more?

Glancing over at Dakari, I could tell the incident that had happened the day before with the mean cop was still weighing heavily on his mind. He was there but not there. He was seated but somewhere else. He was with us in body only. When I finally got his attention, I put my hands on my chin and gestured up to the sky. He slightly smiled, yet I knew he wasn't himself.

Sitting and waiting for my name to be called, I flashed back to a few days before, and sadness came over my face as well. I had been at Tad's graduation, and everything was going great. I was sitting with his family. They were all very proud, as was I. Then out of nowhere, his grandmother passed out. She had a heart attack right there, and unfortunately, unlike my grandfather a few months back, she didn't make it.

I remember watching her not three feet in front of me.

All her kids around her. Tad's mom was one of ten, and all of them were present for his big day. Sadly, it ended up being his grandmother's farewell.

Her last words were, "Calling my name. Love y'all. I hear Him calling my name."

As I became emotional thinking of Tad's grandmother, my silly friend, Lynzi, did a crazy thing. She folded one of the programs into an airplane and threw it my way. It landed right in my face. When I looked up, she had a grin, pointing towards the stands. My inward tears turned into a smile. It was Tad, and in everything he had going on, he was there. He had come to share in my day and because I saw him, I felt ready to accept my diploma.

I was so proud of my girl, Dymond. Valedictorian, on her way to Howard with a full paid scholarship. Against the odds she had done it. And her last words to our senior class that day were so challenging.

"You know," Dymond began. "The projects . . . black . . . poor . . . uneducated parents. When the world says you can't because of your circumstances and your situation, rise above it. Folks, I did. I stand here before my class, not bragging that I'm here, but happy that I'm here because I worked hard for it. Days I studied extra hard to be here, and as we take it up another notch, those of us going to college, remember to work hard for what you want. And don't let anyone kill your dreams."

She received a standing ovation. So she should have. Not only did she work hard, but she motivated me several times to stay in the books rather than go to the mall. All four of us special friends were smart, but she was naturally gifted, and I was so proud of her. Proud that she had defeated the odds.

Dr. Franklin went up to the podium and said, "Now you

guys go out into the world. Make something of yourselves. This young lady just stood here and told you 'no excuses.' Results, man, results. Several of your classmates aren't even sitting here today. Don't fall victim to your circumstances. Rise above them, no matter what they are. This is only a milestone, a first step to where and what you can be. Do all, be all, take all you've learned here and soar. Higher than anyone else ever expects you to. And know that we're behind you. You can always come here for encouragement. To the graduating class of Lucy Laney High School—be great!"

"Payton Autumn Skky" was announced over the loud-speaker.

That was me. I stepped across in a daze. Was this really real? Was this moment finally here? Was I about to graduate?

I looked towards heaven and silently said, *Some things in life we don't deserve. I know I worked hard, but because You were here with me, this moment is here and it's real and it's mine, and I thank You for it. I know You'll be with me next year as I go to college. I just pray I don't leave You. 'Cause just like the "Footprints" prayer, sometimes when I look back on my high school years, and I only saw one set of footprints, turns out You were carrying me, Lord. But now I'm standing here beside You about to accept a diploma and embrace it as my own.*

I looked then at Dr. Franklin and knew life was good. I wasn't dreaming. My principal was most definitely calling my name.

3

Spoiling the Fun

"Put a smile on that face," I said to Dakari after we marched out. "Smile . . . smile. You're too cute to frown."

I thought my last sentence would make him smile. I was wrong. Dakari was out of it.

"I'm cool . . . I'm cool," he replied still with a sad face.

Bam came up and jumped on his back. That totally changed Dakari's somber mood. I was elated to see him finally enjoying the big day, and not letting horrible experiences interrupt the joy of the moment. Dymond came up with her lips all poked out because Fatz wasn't able to be a part of all this. Lynzi, Rain, and I tried everything silly to make her smile as we took off our caps and gowns, but she refused to be happy.

All of a sudden somebody tickled her. When she turned around, she was overjoyed to see Fatz. That was really cool of him to come and support her even though it had to be embarrassing for him not to march with us. Tyson's graduation was the next day, and it was nice to have him among us to celebrate in our joy.

Tad and Tyson came over and gave Rain and me big hugs. The guys had gotten together to come up with a surprise for Rain and me.

We couldn't wait to find out what it was. Before the four of us could exit, my mom put a halt on my plans, and told me that I needed to celebrate with my family. She could tell in my eyes that didn't settle with me, but I could tell by the look in hers that it was going to be her way and not mine, even on my big night.

"Why don't you just invite your friends to come over, and that way we could have a compromise party here?"

All my friends had their plans, but maybe I could convince them to come over to my place for at least an hour or so, and then we could move on and do some other things.

"OK, we'll meet you at the house," I said to my mom.

"No, sweetie, you need to ride with your cousin. She came all the way for your graduation. You can see your friends at the house. I mean, let's be a gracious host now. Come on."

I was so angry inside. How dare my mom tell me that I couldn't ride with my boyfriend or my girlfriends to my own house? Truth be told, I didn't even like Pillar. Though we were getting along, it wasn't a loving relationship. And to make me ride home with her on my night just didn't seem right.

Huffing, I said, "Y'all please come to the house. I gotta baby-sit my cousin. I'll just see y'all there, OK?"

"Cool," Dymond voiced.

Rain said, "Yeah."

"Alright, we'll swing by," Lynzi uttered.

I walked back over to my family and received several hugs from proud folks.

"Hey, Payton," Dymond called out to me.

27

"Grandma, I'll be right back."

Dymond and I went over to her I said, "Yeah, what's up?"

"Who's the white chick?"

"What are you talking about?"

"Over there with your family. Yeah, who's the white girl?"

"Girl, she's not white. That's my cousin. The cousin I just said I had to baby-sit."

Dymond questioned, "Your cousin?"

"She's mixed. Long story. I tell you later."

"That's her cousin, y'all," Dymond turned around and told the whole group.

From their looks nobody believed her either. I don't know why it's so hard to believe. African-American families are a rainbow of colors, in various shades of brown. Some so light that you can't see the brown at all. In the case of my cousin, she just looks like she needs a serious tan.

Tan or no tan, I could tell from their reactions that this was going to be interesting. I walked back over to my family, and Pillar pulled me on my arm.

"Your friends, why are they staring at me?" she said in a distasteful manner.

"I told them you were mixed, and I guess they don't believe me," I said rudely and tugged my arm away.

She defended, "I hate that. Everyone is mixed, Payton."

"What are you talking about?" I asked. "Both my parents are black."

"And both of your parents have different genes that were mixed together to create you. I hate being called 'mixed.' Everybody is mixed," Pillar retorted.

I blew her off by saying, "Yeah, whatever."

Why was my mom watching me? She looked straight at me and mouthed, "Be nice." Seemed like this was my worst nightmare. My mom cared more about making my cousin happier than she did about me wanting to enjoy my graduation night. I thought to myself, *I only have to put up with this for a little while. I'll go home, smile, and leave with my friends.*

I was at home for what seemed like five hours, and none of my friends arrived. Actually, when I looked at the clock it had only been about forty-five minutes, but the torture of entertaining my rotten cousin was making me miserable. The phone rang in my room, and I dashed from the family room to grab it.

Before my answering machine picked up, I said, "Hello! Hello," almost out of breath. "This is the graduate; who am I speaking to?"

"This is the other graduate," Dy said.

Rain echoed, "And the other graduate."

Then Lynzi repeated, "And the other graduate. We got you on the speaker. Heyyyy!"

"Where are y'all?" I said to my girlfriends.

Lynzi replied, "Girl, we in my car driving over to Bam's house. His mama's barbecuing, and he don't have no relatives at his house. You know what I'm saying?"

"So, what's up? You guys saying y'all not coming?" I asked, with disappointment.

"Exactly, we're not coming," Dy explained without caring about my feelings.

"Just take care of whatever you got to take care of there, and swing on over to his house," Lynzi cut in.

Mad, I voiced, "Yeah . . . whatever. Y'all ain't even right."

"Yo' mama the one got you entertainin', not us," Dymond reminded.

"Well, somebody's at my door," I said as I heard the doorbell ringing. "Well, all right, I'll check with y'all later. Don't have too much fun without me."

"See, now you ain't right. You don't want us to have fun," Lynzi said as she called me out.

"You're right . . . you're right. I'm wrong. Y'all have a good time."

"You know we won't have too much fun 'til you get there. Quit trippin'," Dymond voiced.

"Thank you," I said, being a baby.

I didn't get to open my door. Because I was detained by my phone call, my cousin opened it. Standing behind her, a stroke of jealousy went up my spine. She was so pretty. So absolutely gorgeous. Staring at her was making me sick. She was so beautiful, I couldn't stand it, with her long, black hair hanging almost to her feet. Well, maybe not *quite* that long, but it sure was beautiful, and it sure wasn't my hair. The way it flipped as she opened the door and flirted with my guy was too much to bear.

"Oh, I got it," I said to her. "It's for me."

"Don't be rude." Pillar stepped back in front of me and batted her eyes to the fine stranger before her. "Introduce me to this handsome guy—no . . . no. I can introduce myself."

"Why are you pushing me?" I asked her.

"You have to excuse my cousin. It seems she doesn't want me to meet her friends. I'm Pillar, and you, fine gentlemen, are whom?" she breathed, too close to him, as far as I was concerned.

Tad kind of laughed. You could tell he was flattered. He was blushing.

I was angry.

"Tad. Tad Taylor."

"Well, come on in," she said, putting her arm through his.

Though she was only a junior, she acted as if she was ten years older or something. Like this was her house instead of mine and he was her guy, instead of mine. Even when we were kids she liked to show off. Though I thought she had changed, maybe I was too abrupt in making that assumption.

Father, I prayed silently, *help me, because Pillar is absolutely getting on my last nerves. I realize Tad and I aren't completely committed to each other anymore, but it's a given that he's mine and not hers. By the looks of things, I'd say she wants him.*

So please help me before I hurt her. I know it's wrong. I know it's wrong to feel like this, but at least I can admit my weaknesses. I just need Your strength to control myself.

Although I prayed, I couldn't contain the anger that was rising inside of me like an over-flowing sink. When I witnessed my cousin put her arm around Tad's waist, I lost it. Though he moved instantly, her gesture took me over the edge.

"OK, what's up? You got insecurities? I mean, what's going on with you, Pillar? Why you gotta try to come on to my guy? What's up?"

"No . . . it's OK," Tad cut in and said.

"It's not OK. I don't appreciate this. She's disrespecting me in my own house."

"Well, if this offends you, dearie, then I'm totally sorry. I was just being cordial to your date. I'll leave since I can see I'm not wanted here," she said with fake emotion.

As she stormed away, Tad looked at me with slight disappointment. I wasn't even trying to explain to him that my cousin was full of bull. I thought he'd be able to see through her and know that. Yeah, I could tell he was mad at me.

"What . . . what? You have something to say to me? What?" I told Tad bluntly.

"I just thought you had a little bit more compassion, especially for a family member. Why are you so mean? You don't have to worry about anybody taking me away from you. Was that it? Do you think I was going to fall for your cousin, just like that?"

Sighing, I said, "No. It's not even that. You just don't know my cousin, so don't try to defend her. Don't try to make me seem like some bad guy 'cause I don't want her flirting with my boyfriend."

"Oh, so I'm your boyfriend?"

"Don't change the subject. I know we haven't worked through what we are to each other, but you're sure more mine then you are hers, OK? That's really all I'm tryin' to say. My mom's on my case about me being all friendly with her, and now you're on my case. I can't take it either, it's suppose to be MY night. I'm not suppose to be baby-sitting my cousin, who practically wants to be me. She's ruining my night," I lashed out.

Tad said, "You go calm down. I'm going to go check on her."

"Yeah, that makes perfect sense, Tad. Why don't you go check on her, and let your crazy girlfriend calm down?"

"Umm . . . you said it again. My girlfriend, huh?"

"Well . . . you know! Whatever," I yelled.

Although I was furious, he was making me laugh. Deep down in my soul, I guess I did still think of him as my guy. Although we were back and forth in our relationship, I wanted him to still be mine through it all. Through the disappointments and the confusion, I wanted him to still be mine.

My telephone rang again, so I dashed to my room once more. It was my girls again, on the speaker.

"Deja vu, huh, y'all? Y'all miss me? Can't even have any fun 'til I get there."

"Well, don't flatter yourself, but it's pretty close," Dymond said.

"When you coming?" Lynzi yelled. "Bam's mama got a spread. What's up? When you coming?"

"There's no alcohol," Rain yelled.

"That's good," I said. "That's really good."

"Somebody probably drinking somethin' somewhere, though. Don't trip. Don't be naive," Lynzi commented.

"Why don't y'all just come by here? My mom is trippin'. Tad is trippin'. Ugh! Just come swoop me up. Just take me away, please."

"Come swoop you? We can't leave this party."

"Well, we already out getting some more hot dogs; we might as well just go on by," Rain said.

"Thanks, sweetie. Thanks! Thanks! Y'all come get me, please."

"Alright, but you better be ready," Lynzi said.

"Cool. I'll be ready; y'all just hurry up."

I had to figure out a way to get Tad home, Pillar to sleep, and my mom's permission to let me leave. When I went downstairs, Tad was laughing and having a great time with my cousin. My mom was entertaining my family.

Soon as my grandpa saw me, he cheered, "The graduate. Yea!"

People started clapping and everybody started hugging me. Though it was nice, now was not the time to hold me up. I had places to go, things to do, and people to see. Being with my family was not part of the plan. Though I did wanna spend time with Tad, I didn't think he would wanna hang out with my friends. After all, he was still kind of down about his grandmother, and my friends have never really been his crew. I figured maybe tomorrow he and I could hang out, talk, and enjoy things.

"Tad, could I see you?"

He threw up a finger as if to say hold up a second. He was trippin'. I was calling him. Anything Pillar had to say couldn't be as important as what I had to say.

"Tad, please come here," I whined.

"Yeah, what's up?" he questioned.

"Um, I just . . . wanna thank you for coming over and . . . I'll see you tomorrow? Your family needs you. Sorry I didn't make it to the funeral. But I know you need to get going."

"What do you mean? I'm not getting ready to go. You don't have to rush me. I know you're concerned about me and all the stuff going on with my family right now, but they're fine. Mom's wanted me to get out of the house. I'm straight hanging out with your folks. It's taking my mind off of things. Yeah, I'm straight. Thanks," he said as he kissed me on the cheek.

OK, that didn't work, I thought to myself. *What am I going to do?* I walked with him back over to Pillar, and asked her for help upstairs.

"You want my help? For what? You never want my help for anything," she retorted.

"Well, I'm trying to be nice," I responded in a sweet-sounding tone.

"I'm enjoying talking to Tad. Is that OK with you? Do I have to get your permission for everything?" she said, getting loud with me.

"Whatever! Whatever. It's not that serious; I just asked for your help."

"Oh, you really do want my help? Cool. I'll be right back," she turned over to Tad and said.

When we reached the stairs I whispered, "Well, it's not really that I want your help. I just kinda wanted to tell you that, um, my friends are coming to get me, 'cause I'm going over to a graduation deal . . ."

"You going to a party? Oh, cool, I wanna go. Sign me up."

"No, no, no. Not really a party. Not really a party. We just gonna kinda celebrate, but you don't have to go, girl. You stay and enjoy the family."

Before I could continue to convince my cousin that this wasn't an affair she'd want to attend, Dymond, Lynzi, and Rain were in my house, mixing and mingling with my family.

"Good to see you, ladies! Payton told me you all decided to go somewhere else," my mom told them.

"Oh, we just came to pick up Payton, and take her back to where we were, Mrs. Skky," Dymond said, trying to be polite, yet not knowing that I didn't want her to mention it at all. She totally blew everything.

"Oh, that's why you wanted me to leave," Tad whispered in my ear.

"Nooo," I said to him. "No. No. No. Don't misunderstand."

34

"Yeah, right. I'll catch you later. Have fun with your friends. They're more important to you. Wouldn't want to let them down."

He grabbed his coat and headed for the door.

"Payton, how did you think you were gon' leave with all this company sitting here?" my mother asked.

"Girl, you didn't check with yo' mama," Lynzi hit me in the arm and said on the sly.

"Why don't you go'n head and let that child hang out with her friends?" my grandma interjected. "We alright. It's her big night. Let her go have some fun."

"Well, what am I going to do if she leaves?" Pillar said.

"Oh, I'm sure the girls don't mind taking you, Pillar," my mom invited.

"Yeah, um, sure. She can come," Rain said in a hesitant voice.

The three of them looked at me, as if they wished they had never stopped to pick me up. In doing so, they had gotten more than they bargained for. I felt bad, but I guessed I deserved it. Tad walked out. Pillar was joining us. My mom was upset. I was leaving my company. My friends were mad because someone else was crashing the party, and I was absolutely miserable.

This wasn't how I imagined my graduation night, everything upside down. It was pretty safe to say I wasn't enjoying myself. I couldn't necessarily blame it all on my cousin, though deep down I wanted to pin my messed-up night on her. Truthfully, a big part of me felt that she was spoiling the fun.

4

Trying Too Hard

*T*ry. Just try to deal with having my cousin with us. I know this isn't what you bargained for, but, please . . . I'm in a jam," I said to my three girlfriends as I pulled them aside.

"You're asking a lot, and we don't even know this girl. This white chick . . . what's up? Why she gotta come?" Dymond honestly asked.

"You know that's her cousin," Rain explained to Dymond.

Dy realized, "Oh, yeah. That's right. You told me that at graduation. But Pay . . . she didn't look like you, me, or nobody black."

"I know she's your family and all, but that's on you. I mean, we shouldn't have to put up with it. We don't even know her," Lynzi whined.

They were so right, and even though she was my family, I was fed up with Pillar. And out of everyone, I was probably the one who didn't want her with us the most. However, I couldn't let on to that because then my mom would make me stay home with my cousin.

I gave my friends the puppy-dog eyes, and they were all like OK; whatever; yeah, sure. They didn't say it, but I knew they were going to let her go.

"Thanks, y'all! Thanks!" I said as I got excited.

I went up to my mom and politely asked her if I could have a moment. I wanted to be an adult about this. I didn't want to rant and rave and fly off the handle, because even though I felt that my mom had pushed my cousin on me, there was a diplomatic way to express it. Maybe another time may have been appropriate, but because I was so emotional, I knew I needed to get my feelings out immediately.

"Sweetheart, your friends are waiting on you. Why don't you just go with your friends and we can talk when you get back, maybe tomorrow or something," my mom said calmly, as she brushed off my request.

Though I wanted to press the issue, though I wanted to tell my mom what I truly thought, and though I wanted to just go off, I said, "Yes, ma'am. Tomorrow's good."

All the way on the ride over to Bam's house, neither Rain, Dymond, Lynzi, nor I said one word. Pillar, however, was going on and on and on about some of everything that probably none of us heard. When we pulled up to Bam's house, however, was when we all responded to her question.

My cousin probed, "Who is that cute guy in front of that house? I don't usually date black guys, but in his case, I can make an exception."

The way she'd been flirting with Tad earlier, I wouldn't have known she wasn't into dating black guys. Inwardly I chuckled. She was trippin'.

"You don't date black guys? What do you date . . . mixed guys?" Lynzi joked.

Pillar, being the scatterbrain that she is, didn't even pick up on Lynzi's sarcasm.

"I'm sure she only dates white guys," Dymond said in a mean voice.

I wondered why she was mad. I wondered why my cousin dating white guys would bother her. I mean, why should we care whoever she dates, but Dymond definitely had a problem. One that I wanted to address.

"Yeah, most of my boyfriends have been white. I go to a mostly white school, but that guy . . ."

"Which one?" Dy cut her off.

"Right there."

"That guy," Dymond laughed. "Payton, you see the guy she's pointing at?"

"Who cares?" I said out loud. "She can date whoever she wants, like whoever she wants, and see whoever she wants."

"Oh, really," Lynzi joined in and said. "You must not see who she's talking about."

I didn't know why my friends were trippin'. I knew it couldn't have been Tad; first of all, he'd gone home. He'd be the only person I'd . . .

As I thought through those words myself, I realized that wasn't true. That wouldn't be the only person I'd care about Pillar not liking. Surely it couldn't be Dakari. Well, it was. Pillar was checking out Dakari. Right before my eyes, walking towards our car was Mr Graham.

"Well, let me out," Pillar yelled.

Because I told my friends that I didn't care, they aggravated the situation.

"Dakari! Dakari," Lynzi said as she went up to him and grabbed his arm. "Got somebody that we want you to meet. This is Pillar. Pillar, meet Dakari Graham. He was a big time football star at our school."

"Hi," she said in a bad impression of Marilyn Monroe. "Let me give you a hug, graduate."

She was such a big flirt, it was making me absolutely sick. When he smiled and hugged her back really tight, I got a little upset. I jumped out of the car, slammed the door, and went into the party. My lips were poked out the whole time. Pillar was carrying on with Dakari like she had known him a long time. My friends noticed my somber mood.

Lynzi said, "I thought you didn't care. Sure seems like you care to me."

"Lynzi, why you rubbing it in? I don't know if I do care, okay? I just . . . I just . . . Ugh!"

I got up and went to the bathroom. I splashed water on my face, looked in the mirror, and said to myself, "What's up with you, chick? The brother wanted you back. You didn't want him; you wanted another dude. Now you don't know if you want that dude or this one. Ugh. What's wrong with me? I'm not satisfied with anything."

"Payton, could you let me in, please? We need to talk. Payton, could you . . . could you let me in, please?"

"Who is it? Hello . . . I'm in the bathroom."

"Well, are you using it?"

"That's none of your business," I said to the person whose voice I didn't recognize.

"Just a few minutes of your time, please. It's me, Starr. Please."

"Starr Love? What does she want?" I said to myself in the mirror. "What does she want with me? I don't hardly have time for her drama."

I opened the door and she came in. Although we had gotten past a lot of the drama that had made us common enemies, she still wasn't my bosom buddy. After all, she had come to our school at the beginning of the year and stolen my boyfriend.

"Starr, what is it?" I said, not rude, but not warm. "What's wrong with your eyes?" I asked, looking at the round red circles.

"It's . . . it's . . . it's Dakari. He's . . . he's dating a white girl. I mean I . . . I don't . . . I don't . . . I don't understand."

"If you mean the girl out there whom he's with now, she's not white. She's mixed, and she's my cousin. I'm sure she's just tryin' to make me jealous. Don't sweat it. No big deal."

"Now that I think about it, you seem jealous. You're here in the bathroom," Starr called me out.

"Yeah, right. Whatever! I'm not even hardly jealous. Look at you. You're the one. I thought you were dating some college guy. What do you care about what Dakari's doing anyway?"

She taunted, "Why do you seem so angry? Why you acting so mean? You're always such a sweet lil' girl."

"Little? I think we are the same age."

"You know what I mean. Seriously, maybe you need to check your feelings. I'm a good judge of character, and I think something is there."

She was right. I was jealous and I didn't know how to admit it myself. I was being evil, mean, nasty, everything that wasn't me because my cousin was taking over my space. Yeah, Dakari wasn't mine. I could possibly deal with losing him to Starr once again. Point was, I just didn't want Pillar to have him.

"Your cousin? Well, what are you going to do about it? She's talking to my man. We need to fix this. Correction—you need to fix this because you brought her here."

"Quit trippin'," I told her. "Dakari is grown. We all are. Whoever he wants to be with is whoever he wants to be with. If he wants to be with you, he'll be with you. If he wants to talk to my cousin, then let him do so. He'll find out the hard way."

That sounded good, I thought to myself. *But was it true?* I thought again, *that sounded good.*

"I know he'll listen to you, Payton. I know he'll listen to you," she walked out of the bathroom saying, without giving me a chance to speak.

First of all, I didn't know why she thought Dakari would listen to me. A long time ago, when I wanted him to continue being my boyfriend instead of hers, he never listened to me. He dumped me, as a matter of fact. Why would she think he'd want to listen to me now?

"I don't have time for this," I said to myself in the mirror. "Look at me; I'm going crazy. These folks are stressin' me."

Before I could calm down, there was a knock on the door. Granted, I had been in here a while, but if folks see the light on they should be patient. Surely I could have expected not to be disturbed.

"Someone's in here!" I yelled because obviously whoever it was didn't get the point.

Nothing was said by the person on the other side. There was just a repeated knock. And then an annoying knock.

In frustration, I gasped, opening the door, "Yes?"

It was Dakari, looking as cute as ever. No Pillar. No Starr. Just Dakari, leaning up against the door waiting for me to invite him in. I was going crazy because I couldn't deny what I was feeling. There was something. Something that I couldn't shake. Something that I couldn't understand. Deep down inside, I knew he was no good for me, but maybe somewhere, I wished that he was.

I had loved, cared, and thought of him for so many years that seeing him this way warmed my soul. Deep inside I felt good. He had found out that my cousin wasn't about all that. He had come to find me, and I felt special.

"You're not saying anything. Yes? Yes? Why are you standing here?" I teased him, knowing I wanted him to admit how much he wanted to find me.

"What are you talking about? You called for me."

"I called for you?" I questioned.

"Yeah. Starr just came and got me and said you needed to see me immediately. So I left your cousin, and I'm standing here."

"What?"

He asked me, "You didn't call for me?"

Dejected and angry, I said, "No. No, I didn't call for you."

I walked out the bathroom. I left Dakari there. I was ready to go, so I went to find Rain.

"Can you take me home?" I asked her with a slight attitude.

"Lynzi drove."

"Whatever! Can you get her keys, and take me? I'm ready to go."

With a dejected face Rain probed, "What's wrong with you?"

"Sorry for snapping. I'm just not in the best mood right now."

"Heyyy cuz. Did I just here you say you're ready to go? You can't leave, the party has just started. Heeyyy!" My no-beat, no-rhythm cousin swayed back and forth to the music.

Dakari walked up and put his arm around Pillar. "I drove. I'll take you and your cousin home. That's cool."

"Ooohh, thanks for taking us home, baby."

Pillar didn't even know Dakari, yet she was already calling him baby. My ears didn't fail me. She called him baby. I wanted to go home bad, but partly because I wanted to get away from the two of them, and now I had to ride with them to get home. This just wasn't my night. My senior graduation night wasn't my night.

"Fine. Whatever. Just take me home," I told Dakari.

"Oh, girls, hugs, hugs, hugs," Pillar said to my friends.

"Girl, no. You better back up," Dymond told her being real.

"Tomorrow. Maybe tomorrow you will get to know me better. We're going to be good friends. Since I'll be here for a few weeks, we'll get to hang out."

"Don't push it," Lynzi told her before walking away.

A few weeks she'd be here. Just hearing her say it was so upsetting, so much so that I felt like I had the flu.

Pillar was sleeping in my room, and I got out of the bed. I couldn't sleep. Not because my night had turned into a disaster, but something inside of me was torn. There was no understanding, no peace, and I couldn't put myself to rest 'til I dealt with some deep issues.

Sipping on some peach passion tea at three o'clock in the morning, I just needed to relax. However, I couldn't so I laid my head down on the table and wiped two trickling tears from my eyes. I tried not to make a lot of noise. I didn't want to disturb anyone. It was too early in the morning for folks to be waking up. Yet, when the hall light came on, I knew I had failed in my attempts to keep the noise down.

Someone stroked my hair. The gentle touch felt so soothing. When I looked up, it was my mom.

"What's wrong, baby?" she asked in a caring voice. "What's wrong?"

She went over and fixed herself a cup of tea and sat down beside me. She didn't rush me to get out what was difficult to keep in. Her concern let me know that she genuinely cared about my frustration, and I wanted to talk to her. We just hadn't had one of those heartfelt chats in a while.

God, let me say the right thing, I thought. Maybe that's why He sent my mom to nestle down with me at the table. He knew I needed her. Maybe she could help me figure out what's really going on.

"Well, I'm not pregnant or anything."

"No, I didn't think that you were. I don't know everything you do, but I respect you as a young woman, and I know you respect yourself. And I know you respect God.

But it's something going on, and I sense it's relationship-oriented because it's really got you emotional. I know you care about people. Is it something to do with that?"

"I think you're right, Mom," I said to her.

"Is it Tad?" she questioned.

That was it. When she said his name, I realized my dilemma. I had to fix this and just maybe talking it out would help.

"Mom, I care about two guys. I think I'm in love with two guys, and I know you think I'm young and all that, but I still care about Dakari, and I know I care about Tad. And whenever I'm with one of them . . ."

"That's the guy your heart beats for," my mom said as she finished what I couldn't say, but meant.

"Yeah, beats for," I replied. "It's like I'm forcing myself to choose between one or the other so that I'm not like . . . leading one of them on, but just when I think I'm over Dakari, I realize I'm not, and I just . . . I don't know what to do. I don't know what I'm feeling. I don't know what I want. Well, I guess I do know what I want. I want both of them. That's wrong," I told her, being absolutely honest.

"Seems like your focuses are on these young men, and I like both of them, but it seems like you need to concentrate on something more important than boys."

"You mean God?"

"Yes," she said quickly, "I mean God. You don't have to know how you feel right now about Tad or Dakari or any of that stuff. But what you need to know and be sure of is that God is guiding your life, because if you're in His will He'll direct you to that boyfriend, that friend, that companion, and one day the man that's going to be your mate for life. Trust God for those answers, not yourself. Don't depend on Payton to know who it is, because it might not be either of them, and for this time, who knows, maybe God has something better for you. Something neither one of them can fulfill and/or help you accomplish."

"I know. I just wish . . . I just wish . . ."

"Think about what I said tonight, sweetie," my mom uttered as she placed her hand on my wrist. "God needs to be in control of your life. You don't have to figure things out. Give your woes to Him. Relax. You just graduated. As you say, stop stressin'. It'll all come together; you're just trying too hard."

5

Embracing Beyond Belief

*T*wo weeks had passed from the whole graduation fes-
tivities, and Pillar was still around and ever getting on
my nerves. Everywhere I went she had to go. Everything I
did, she had to do. It even got to a point that everything I
ate, she wanted to eat, and every person I talked to, she had
to say, "Hello." There was no clear-cut line on what was
mine and what was hers. Although she's my cousin, I didn't
want her to be my clone.

My parents had fully taken her in as their own child.
Though she was only with us for a month, she was getting the
royal treatment, and it seemed as if I was getting booted out. I
couldn't wait to go to college, so I wouldn't have to have any
more direction on what I had to do.

"Yeah, we'll be ready in ten minutes. That's cool. OK. Sure.
Bye," Pillar said as she hung up the phone, tryin' to talk like
me.

"Who were you talking to?" I asked her entering my room
and being caught off guard that my cousin had made plans.

Seemingly the plans she made were for the both of us. "Who were you talking to?"

"Just your girlfriends. Our girlfriends," Pillar joked.

"What are you talking about, OUR girlfriends?"

"Your friends. Our friends. I mean Rain, Dymond, and the other chick."

"You were talking to Rain, Dymond, and Lynzi?"

"Yeah, Lynzi. I always forget her name. I need to hang out with her more. Maybe that will help me remember. Anyway, they're on their way over to get us," my cousin responded.

"What?" I said, absolutely bewildered.

I had been trying to get my girlfriends to accept my cousin for two weeks, and they weren't having it. I couldn't understand now why all of a sudden they were going to pick her up and she was talking to them on the phone like they were tight. Something wasn't right.

"So you called them, right?" I asked, trying to figure out how this happened. "You called my friends?"

"Yeah, I called them."

"Well, how did you get their number?"

Pillar sighed, "You've got it on your speed dial. I've seen you press it a million times."

"So you just called up my friends," I asked for clarity, "and asked them to come and pick us up? So basically you just pushed yourself on them."

"I was trying to make plans for us. Don't be annoyed with me. I was doing you a favor. We've been sitting in this house all week not doing anything. Let's go out and have some fun. I'm not going to be here too much longer. I do want to enjoy myself. I don't want to be up under you all day. I wanna let my hair down and have some fun."

She had some nerve. Making plans with my friends just because she didn't want to be up under me. That was a trip. That was a real trip. My cousin, who was practically taking over my space, pounced up and went off to get dressed. Even if I'd objected, I don't think she would've cared. It was going to be her way and that was the way it was. I could either go or stay. It was clear that she no longer needed me.

However wrong the feeling, I couldn't shake my resentment towards her. Staring at the adorable pale pink short set she was going to put on, I wanted to cut holes in it, burn it, mess it up, shrink it, something. I didn't want her to put it on and look even cuter than me. Imagining her in it would be too . . .

What am I thinking? I told myself. *I can't be crazy. I can't even try to act crazy, be crazy, do crazy things. She can't get to me like this. I won't let her stress me out.*

"Oooh, girl, your cousin is so cool," Lynzi said to me later that afternoon when we were in the park.

"For a chick who's half white," Dymond explained, "she's real. She's down with us. You know what I'm sayin'. She's pretty cool."

"I agree with you, Lynzi. I like 'ole Piller."

My best friend Rain and Pillar had gone to Krystal's to get us some burgers. It was ironic; just a week ago I was telling them to give my cousin a chance. Just let her hang with us some more and they'd find she was cool. Though I said this and that, and now that they were embracing what I said, it didn't feel right. I could've kicked myself for pushing it. They were talking like she was a part of the crew, saying stuff like "Where we going next?" Trying to make plans for the rest of the day. My stomach was turning.

"What's your problem?" Lynzi called me out. "It seems like you have an attitude or something. Like you don't want your cousin to hang out with us. I mean, what's up with that?"

"I don't know myself. I'm just tired. I mean, it's the weekend. Do we have to keep going and going and going like the daggone Energizer bunny? Can't we just chill out, go our separate ways? You guys are planning stuff all night long. What's up with that?" I questioned my friends.

"Well, we're not tired. Since you have the energy of a great-grandmother, why don't you go home and rest? We're going out, and your cousin's old enough to make up her own mind."

"Cool. Fine. Whatever," I angerly lashed back before stomping off.

"Good," Lynzi yelled. "That's cool. Be that way. You're the one who'll miss out."

From the corner of my eye I could see her walk away. Invisible steam was shooting fiercely from my ears. I was too through. Yet I didn't understand why I was so angry.

"Lord, what's wrong with me?" I said later that night as I lay in my bed, finally by myself. Pillar did go out with my friends, and I couldn't stand it. And because I couldn't stand it, I was alone. Something didn't seem right with that, and I knew only God could help me. Before I heard a word from the Lord, my ringing phone interrupted my prayer. Though I didn't want to answer it, being annoyed by the ring, I finally said . . .

"Hello!"

"Payton, is this a bad time?" a sweet voice answered back.

"Shayna Mullen? I'm so sorry. I didn't mean to sound so harsh. How are you doing?"

"Well, I was gonna ask how you were doing, but it seems maybe you're not too good. Are you OK, Payton?"

"It's just a whole bunch of stuff going on that I can't explain."

With compassion she stated, "You know, I've been think-ing about you a lot. Been meaning to get around to calling you and all that stuff. A lot has been going on with my husband and me. We're having . . ."

"Are things OK?" I questioned with concern.

"Uh, good stuff has been going on."

I cut in and said, "A baby!"

"Yeah," she said.

"Oh, how exciting! Congratulations!"

"Thank you," she said. "But even with everything going on, I still have been thinking about you so much. Tell me what's up with you. Lady, what's really going on?"

It was nice to know that she cared so much about me in her own joy. Just knowing she couldn't get me off her mind meant so much. Even though we hadn't truly started our discipleship yet, I did feel a warm connection. I knew the stuff she wanted to know about me was from her heart. Not to be nosy or anything—it's just that she cared.

Maybe God had answered my prayer. Maybe the ringing phone wasn't a distraction. Maybe He allowed her to call me for such a time as this, and I was going to tell all and be as honest as I could so I could receive some help. Covering up my true feelings and making my life seem rosy wasn't going to help any. She asked for the deep stuff, and I was determined to give it to her. I could only hope she wouldn't think too bad of me. If so, oh well. That was a risk I needed to take.

"I don't know . . . I just . . . I'm kinda mad with myself right now," I revealed.

"Explain some more to me. What do you mean, you're disappointed in yourself?"

"I don't know. It's just my feelings, my thoughts, my anger."

Shayna quizzed, "What are you mad at? Do you know, Payton?"

"For starters . . . my cousin. Oh, I'm so mad at my cousin."

"Tell me about it."

"Well, her name is Pillar. She's a year younger than me. She's gorgeous, and she's taking over my life."

"What do you mean, she's taking over your life?" Shayna asked in disbelief.

"I mean just that. My mom wants to please her more than she wants to please me. All her stuff is all over my room. I don't know. I'm just kinda tired of her. I know maybe that's not right, but that's just the way I feel."

I really liked Shayna. She wasn't judging me. She wasn't telling me that I was totally wrong, which even I knew I was. Yet, I just didn't understand why. She just kinda listened and actually felt sympathy for me, and I appreciated that. However, before we got off the phone she did tell me that I needed to look deep inside myself and see why I really had a problem with my cousin.

After hanging up the phone, I examined that whole issue. Was there something else that was so hidden inside of me, a deeper reason I couldn't stand being around her? I had to think about it and hope to find out what was really going on. Though I thought I knew, maybe I didn't.

No sooner than I could collect my thoughts did the phone ring once again. This time, not knowing who it could be and not wanting to be rude, though I wasn't in the best of moods, I answered with dignity. It was my friend, Tad Taylor. My friend. My friend. He was driving in the area and asked if he could stop by. Such a gentleman he was, and maybe just the gentleman I needed.

I met him outside. Since walking the neighborhood was one of our favorite things to do and since it was such a nice night, we decided to stroll.

"Flowers? Who are the flowers for?" I asked Tad as he stood before me with a bunch of pink, white, and yellow carnations.

"They are for you. Who else, but for you?"

"Okay, hold up a second. I'll be right back so we can take a walk," I told him.

Flowers? I wonder what the flowers are for, I pondered when I got inside. I knew this gesture meant he had something important to say to me, but what? We were on shaky ground.

Mainly because I messed up. Now our relationship was unsure. And I thought it only right to end things and just be friends with Tad. However, I couldn't speculate on what he wanted. So I hurried back to him so he could explain what he was thinking.

We'd walked halfway around the block in silence. If there was dirt, we would have been kicking it up with our feet. We were looking down at the ground instead of at each other.

"Something's wrong," I finally got the courage to say to him. "What is it? You're thinking heavy on something. Let me in. What is bothering you, Mr. Tad Taylor?"

I stopped the walking and grabbed both of his hands. He looked at me. He finally looked at me, eye-to-eye.

He said with a serious face, "I miss you."

"I miss being around you too," I told him, mesmerized by the moment.

"No. No, it's deeper than that. I know it's deeper than that. I really, really miss you. I miss holding you in my arms. I miss you as my girlfriend. I miss all that stuff. Payton, you're my girl. I mean, you were my girl. I just can't shake that. Basically, I just wanna know what I need to do to make you mine again."

I couldn't believe what I was hearing. Not that I didn't want to hear it, but I couldn't believe that this guy was saying these words to me. With all the drama that I put him through. I couldn't believe it was me that he was still embracing beyond belief.

6

Invading
Wrong Territory

I don't know, Tad," I said to him after taking in his wanting to be with me. "I'm flattered. I can't believe you still want us."

"Why is it so hard to believe?" he said as he clutched both of my hands. "Don't you still want us, too?"

I didn't remove my hands from his, yet a part of me wanted to. I couldn't look him in the eyes to give him my response because a part of me didn't want to say that I was confused.

So I looked toward the sky and uttered, "I don't know what I want, and until I do, I'm not going to play with you. Can't we just remain friends?"

I didn't know what he was going to say, but what he said stunned me tremendously. I wasn't expecting the response I got. My face displayed shock.

"I don't know."

For a guy who's always so sure of himself, hearing him say "I don't know" wasn't enough for me. His usual response was either a yes or no. It wasn't an "I don't know" question.

It had to be one or the other. Either we weren't going to be friends or we were. He needed to figure it out, and I needed him to figure it out quickly.

"Why is it so hard for us to stay friends? I mean . . . what's the big deal?"

"The big deal is that I want to be more than that. The big deal is I don't want you going out with that daggone Dakari joker just because you don't feel like you're tied to me, and then maybe when you feel like it, you call me up and we go out to the movies. No, that's not cool. That's not how it's going to be, and I don't want to give you the feeling that having it that way is cool with me. You know what? It's either all or nothing. Friends? Yeah, call me on the phone; we can talk, but thinkin' you gon' date both of us . . . I'm not down with that."

He had called me out before I could really admit it to myself. That's exactly what I wanted to do, As I noticed his eyes start watering, I could have assumed it was from allergies, but being that I knew better, I felt bad. I was hurting a guy that I cared about deeply, and that was never my intention.

I was taking Tad Taylor, a genuinely sweet guy, to a place that he should never be, again. I had done it before when he noticed Dakari kissing what was then his girlfriend. And although I wasn't trying to hurt him, I was successful in doing so.

"I gotta go," he said, full of emotion.

Before I got a chance to say anything, the brother who did own part of my heart was gone, and now I was in a place with Tad that I didn't want to be. *Could this be fixed?* I wondered as I watched him drive away. Only the part of my heart that Tad didn't own knew the answer to that.

"Where you going?" I asked my cousin the next week as she darted around the room getting dressed.

"Dakari is taking me out."

"What?"

"Yeah, he's coming to swoop me up, and we're going out on a date. What's the problem? You staying in again? You better call that Tad guy."

I couldn't say a word. Though I wanted to say plenty, I remained silent. However, this was not cool.

"So who else is going out with y'all?" I probed, finally realizing I did have questions to ask. "It's not just like a date with the two of you, right? I mean, it's going to be other people?"

"Well, other people are going, but it is a date. Lynzi and Bam are going, and Dakari is going with me. Yes, it's a date. Why would you ask that? I'm not just going to hang out with him. I'm going to get to know him."

She better not get to know him too well, I thought to myself. Shoot. This was not a good thing, and Lynzi, she was a trip. She knew that wasn't even right. She knew I still liked Dakari. *What's up with her?*

Pillar had gotten permission from my mom to go out. She just had to be back in by ten. At least I felt somewhat special; my curfew was eleven-thirty only it didn't matter since I wasn't going anywhere. The doorbell rang for Pillar's big evening out. I answered the door because she was still primping. All three of my friends looked at me as if there was no problem with this arrangement. However, my stare, my bold stare, told them that I was totally not happy with this.

"Lynzi, can I speak to you for a sec?"

The guys went downstairs to wait on Pillar. Lynzi and I stepped back outside my front door.

Lashing out, I said, "I thought you'd have my back. I thought you were my friend. What's up with this . . . going on a date with Dakari and Pillar? Settin' them up? I mean . . ."

"Wait a minute. What are you accusing me of? I didn't set this up. She wanted to go out with him. He wanted to go out with her. Bam thought it would be cool to just hang out with them, so we're going. It's not like I encouraged them to be together. See, I always tease you about your feelings for Mr. Graham, and you always say you don't care about him. So why are you trippin' now? You still like the brotha a lot, don't you?"

I was finally at a place where I had to admit my feelings for Dakari to myself, and although I knew the answer was yes, I wasn't quite ready to reveal it. So I just walked away rudely. My friend Lynzi had hurt my feelings by participating in this little Pillar-Dakari evening out. So I, at that moment, didn't care if my ugly ways hurt her. At that time, to me, she deserved it.

"Rolling your eyes, Pay . . . ain't cute, but if it's like that . . . if that's how you wanna play, then, oh, yeah. I'll show you how I can encourage the two of them to get together. You ain't seen nothin' yet."

No response was given to her idle threat. Inside, however, my wild, loose acquaintance Lynzi was getting told off. As I distanced myself from her, I smiled at my thoughts.

I went back inside the house, and Lynzi waited for the three of them outside. When I closed my front door, I didn't know what to do. Should I go down to Dakari and tell him I wanted him back in my life? Or should I let well enough alone, and take the sign that since he wanted to be with someone else, my cousin, no less, then that's the way it should be?

I stood frozen for about six minutes. Before I could make a decision, Dakari was squeezing by me, trying to open the door and exit with Pillar in arm. It was as if I was caged, unable to speak and tell him my innermost thoughts, and he didn't even look my way to see what I was feeling. They just left my home and headed out for a good time. In no way was this a good thing. In no way did I like this. In no way was I happy about Dakari going out with Pillar.

"Lord," I said in sadness, "I don't know what's wrong with me. I don't know what I want. Maybe that's the problem. I should be wanting what You want for me. Just give me strength. Strength to get it together and not be so unhappy. I shouldn't care what Dakari does, but I do, Lord. I do. Help me. Like only You can. In Jesus' name. Amen."

"Oh, my gosh! Oh, my gosh! Do we have a steak?" Pillar yelled as she ran into the kitchen.

She had just come in from her night out, and I had no idea what the problem was. A steak from the kitchen? Was she serious? I'm sure they had gone out to eat. What did she care if we had steak? She was in such a state of panic. Something was wrong.

"What's going on?" I said to her as I nibbled on a peanut-butter-and-jelly sandwich.

She fumbled through the freezer to actually find a steak, a real T-bone steak. As she put it in the microwave to defrost it somewhat, I got up to find out what was going on. She just kept blabbering to herself. I couldn't understand a word.

"Slow down," I finally said. "Tell me what's wrong. You're not making sense."

She grabbed the steak out of the microwave and flew back outside to Bam's car. Curiosity got the best of me, so I followed her. Dakari was holding his head back in the passenger's seat, and he had a severely battered black eye.

"What's going on?" I asked.

Lynzi grabbed me and pulled me over to the side of the car.

"Girl, Dakari had it out with some white guys at the movie theater."

"What? What are you talking about? White guys . . . movies . . . please explain this. I don't understand."

I knew Dakari had a temper, but he was always a lot of talk. I never imagined him to actually get into a physical brawl.

"I don't know. A couple of guys made some comments about the white girl going out with the black guy and all that stuff, and said she was nothing but trash, and all kinds of horrible comments, and we all tried to ignore it for the longest. Then they made comments about Dakari, and he turned around and tackled one of the guys. And then it kinda got unfair quickly, because another guy came in and started swingin', and the next thing we know, Dakari got hit in the eye, and we were all tossed out the movie theater," Lynzi revealed.

"You mean those guys that picked the fight in the first place got to stay in the theater?"

"Naw, they ran away before the police came and stuff, 'cause Dakari wanted to file a report."

Based on what had happened to him on the day before graduation with the cop, I knew that's why he wanted to report it. He was tired of race incidents and people getting away with it. He wanted to take action.

"I don't blame him for wanting to press charges," I said.

"We would've been here sooner, but we had to wait on the cops, and he had to give his report and stuff. I don't know why he had to report it," Lynzi said. "They'll never find those guys."

I wanted to tell her of Dakari's former pain in that area. However, I just let it go. Quickly, I fled to his side to make sure he was all right. Deep down I felt he needed me.

"You okay, baby?" I said as I kneeled at his feet.

Pillar sort of pushed me out of the way and rudely said,

"I got it. I can take care of this. He'll be fine. He was defending me, after all. He'll be fine."

As Pillar stroked his head, anger rose up in me. It was the same tension I felt almost a year ago when Dakari was with another girl, Starr. I hated being torn like this. Liking Tad. Liking Dakari. Not really knowing who I liked the most. However, I knew I felt something for the one with the bruised eye before me, and I couldn't just watch my cousin take over my space, my friend, or my guy.

So, I watched from afar, wanting to change the view before me. However, I just needed something to spark my interference, and when I saw Pillar reach to kiss him, that did it.

"No! No, no, no!" I said as I reached to pull Dakari up from the car and jerk him away from her. "This can't happen like this. No, Dakari. This can't happen."

"What are you talking about? What's up?" he said sort of out of it, probably not even aware that that kiss was coming from her.

I was struggling with a lot of turmoil on the inside. I couldn't believe I was acting as desperate as I was. However, though I knew it was wrong to want a guy so badly, I couldn't fight those feelings.

Without thinking about being sensitive to Dakari's predicament, I selfishly voiced, "I know this probably isn't the right time, but it's just not right that you be with Pillar in any way, a date, anything. I got some stuff going on inside of me, man, that's all about you. I can't stand here and watch her take over. I think I kinda wanna work on us. She's invading wrong territory."

7

Vacationing with Trouble

*J*ust a little trip, huh?" I said to Dakari as I leaned back
in the seat next to him.

"We're going to Columbia. Going to watch the fireworks. I'm going to take you someplace really special. You
deserve it, lady," he boasted.

We had been seeing quite a lot of each other since I
dropped the bomb on him and let him know that the feelings he knew I still had for him were real. Most definitely
real. Every morning before I woke up he called me, and
every night before I went to bed, he was whispering dreamy
words through the phone. That was how it used to be with
Dakari and me. From the tenth grade 'til last summer we
were always chatting over the phone. I miss those talks.

I didn't know where Dakari and I were headed, but at
the time I didn't care. I was too caught up in the feelings.
That familiar feeling for a guy who not only looked so good,
but also talked so right, had apparently never completely left
my heart.

Starr Love had no more power with him. The beautiful girl, who'd won him over because she was giving him what he wanted, was no longer an issue. My cousin, Pillar, whatever it was she was trying to flaunt, he wasn't eyeing. The only person he was looking at was me, and as we drove down the road, he glanced my way and winked. I melted like a chocolate bar left out in the sun.

We talked about the unfortunate incident with the cop. Sadly Dakari admitted that he still dreams about that day. He also told me that he feels that made him an agrier person.

What's he thinking? I wondered as thirty minutes passed by and neither he nor I said anything. Instead of talking we grooved to the beats on the radio. With only fifteen more minutes left 'til we reached our destination, I wanted to say something, but what? What could I say? Could I promise him something I wasn't sure I could deliver on—which was probably what he wanted to hear?

It took me back to almost a year to the day when we were driving to Athens to see his brother play in a college football game. Dakari wanted something from me and I wasn't ready to give it. Right now I wasn't sure I was ready, but this time at least, I wanted desperately to give it.

Though the feeling should have been scary, it wasn't. Though I was unsure, I was calm. Though I didn't know what would happen, I was anticipating a wonderful night. Dakari Ross Graham was with me, and, in every way, I wanted to be with him.

"So, can I ask you a personal question?" he kept his head focused straight on the road, while he turned down the music to speak to me.

Not knowing what I was in for, I said, "Sure. Anything."

"How far did you and yo' boy go?" he asked, getting straight to the point. So straight that I had a crooked look on my face. I wasn't expecting that question, and, boy, did I *not* know what to say. It was such a complex question and

Dakari mentioning Tad made me even more uneasy. Made me feel like I was cheating, which was crazy because Tad and I weren't together. I should have been able to tell Dakari that my former boyfriend believed in abstinence until marriage. For whatever reason, those words didn't come out.

Though Tad and I had broken off our relationship, I knew what we still had, and it was something. I realized that when it came to guys, I was on a roller-coaster ride. One hour up with Tad and the next minute up with Dakari.

"I shouldn't have mentioned him, huh? What's up? You still like him—what? What's going on with you, Payton? Talk to me."

"What do you want me to say? The truth? Because if you do want me to say the truth, Dakari, I don't think you're gonna be satisfied with the answer that I give, because I don't know. Truthfully, I don't know."

"Yeah, right. You know what you feel," he said harshly kinda mad I wouldn't answer him.

"No, really. I don't know. And that's kinda why I wanted to be with you tonight. I wanted to find out. How much of this stuff that's going on in my head for you is suppose to be there. We're going away to school next month. That's a big deal. I don't want to be wishy-washy in my stand."

"In your stand?"

"Well, you know, like who my man is," I said. "When I go to the University of Georgia, if I'm going to say you're my man, then you are my man, and I want us to be committed to each other during our time there."

"We don't need to talk about all this stuff now," he said as he grabbed my hand. "We're getting too worked up about the future, and we don't even know where this present day is going to lead us. Let's just relax, chill, and get reacquainted with one another."

The strip where he turned had nothing but hotels on it. Dakari pulled in the parking lot of one of them. As I sat in the car while he went into the Holiday Inn, I looked up towards the sky.

In denial, I uttered, "OK. This might be wrong . . . OK, it is wrong, but I can't not do this, Lord. So much of me has been thinking 'bout this. Thinking about this guy. Remembering how I even lost him in the first place. Though I've tried to grow from that place, knowing that I never wanted to be with a guy just because he said it was time. I don't know, maybe I'm saying it's time for me to be intimate. I don't know, maybe I do need You to intervene, but, boy, do I not want You to. I'm a horrible person. In advance, I'm sorry."

"Who are you talking to?" Dakari said as he opened the car door.

"Just praying."

Helping me out of the car, he said, "I know you know why I brought you here. But just in case you don't, it's because I love you. I wanna show you that love. If this is too much for you, just tell me now. Tell me and I'll back off."

"No! I want this," I recklessly uttered with little hesitation.

He kissed me slowly and at that point, I felt like putty in his hands. Any which way he wanted to move me, I'd go. He whisked me to room 229. As he opened the door, and the big bed stared at me, the nervousness finally set in. This was the moment of truth. Could I go through with it?

After the loud boom of the door shutting behind us, Dakari took to seducing me. He kissed my neck, my ears, and my lips. The kisses were mesmerizing. I was diggin' the pleasure.

We got there just in the nick of time. The fireworks were about to start as we heard one pop. Luckily, it broke the tight bond between us. Quickly, I broke away from his kisses, went over to the window, and pulled the curtain back.

"It's so pretty," I said to him as bright lights filled the sky.

Dakari came up behind me and once again started pecking my ear. Before I realized what was happening, we had moved from the chair to the queen-sized bed. Weird as it sounds, it was like the bed was talking to me.

"Lay here, Payton, and you'll sin. You better get up now. You better run. You better go. One more second and you won't be pure. You better get up. You better go now," I imagined the bed saying.

Yet, Dakari's embrace was holding me in and I imagined it saying, "I want you. I need you. I love you. Let me show you how much I want to be yours. You didn't answer earlier, baby, but I knew you and Tad hadn't taken that step. I can tell. You're too timid, and I know this is supposed to be my moment. My moment with you. Let's take it now, Payton."

Perplexed! With him—but not there. Scared, but wanting to try, was the situation I had found myself in. As he slowly lifted my shirt, tears began to fall, tumbling down my face because in my spirit I knew what I was doing was wrong. The tears just kept coming and coming and coming, wetting my face and confusing my mind.

Dakari ignored them. He didn't stop. He kept on and kept on pursuing his goal. As if this was a game and he had to score a touchdown. It was weird, but I was caged. I could not speak one word to say no. Yet, "No" was all I wanted to say. Fortunately for me, the phone rang, and it broke my trance.

"I got to get it," I yelled.

"Just let it ring. No one knows we're here."

"No. No. It's my cell phone. I . . . I gotta get it . . . it might be an emergency," I said in a panic, hoping that would make him stop.

When he wouldn't let me get up, I started screaming.

"Get off me!" Finally, the words I wanted to say came out in full force. "No! I don't want this. Get off of me! Now, Dakari—move!"

As I reached for my phone, he pulled me back to him. We were tussling. It was so scary. The guy I knew so well—

or should I say, thought I knew so well—I really did not know at all. He wanted what he said he wanted, and nothing I said or wanted was going to stop him from having his way.

"OK, you trippin'. Do I need to grab the lamp and knock you upside the head? Get off of me, Dakari—now!"

I screamed even loader than before.

"Shh, Payton, you're gonna disturb the other guests. Let's just enjoy ourselves." He tried coaxing me to surrender.

When he inched up a little bit, I put my foot in his chest and pushed back so hard that he was flung across the room. Instantly, I grabbed the phone.

"Hello? Hello? Hello? Hello," I said, out of breath.

"What's wrong with you girl," my brother, Perry, said into the phone.

"Perry. What's up?"

"You OK?" he asked.

"No! Not really."

"Well, you better get back home. Mama and Daddy looking for you, girl."

"What do you mean, looking for me? I thought you had my back?"

"Yeah, I did have your back 'til you gave me a lame excuse. You said you were going over to Rain's house."

"That's a good excuse."

"Yeah, it was, but you must not have told Rain. She came over here looking for you. She said something 'bout wanting to go see a new movie. Mom and Dad are furious."

"Are you serious? What am I going to do?"

Wisely, he suggested, "You better meet me somewhere, because if you come back with Dakari, and you said you were going to be with Rain, you in trouble."

That was an understatement. My parents would flip. I'd be in trouble forever if they caught me with Dakari.

"Well my car's over his house. Mom and Dad are going to kill me."

"You better think of something as you're driving home. You better hurry up too because they 'bout to go out looking for you. I'm serious. I can only stall them for so long."

"Thanks, Perry. Thanks for having my back."

Surprisingly, when I got off the phone Dakari had put back on his shirt and his shoes. He proceeded with frustration to the door. He was ready to take me home. Looking at his face, I could tell he was very disappointed and mad, but shoot, I was angry and upset too. Actually, I was pretty ticked off at him.

He didn't say anything and I didn't say anything. Neither one of us wanted to address the problem. I just composed myself, put on my sandals, and exited out the door.

After being quiet for forty minutes of a forty-five-minute trip, I finally said, "I guess we're good at not saying anything to each other when we drive. Huh?"

"Is that supposed to be a joke?" he said. "I really don't have anything to say. I don't know what you want."

"I can't believe you're mad because I'm not ready!" I told him, honestly.

"Girl, you playin' games. Teasin' folk. Going out to a hotel with me. I mean, what did you think I wanted to do, hold your hand? Let's be real. C'mon. You knew there was more involved, and you led me to believe you were down with it. Then all of a sudden you pull back. I'm supposed to be cool with that? Like yo' lil' other boyfriend. Well, holding hands might be fine for him, but I'm in it for a little bit more than that, and if you can't deliver on more than that, then I'm not the brotha for ya. All this back and forth, you don't know who you like and all that kind of stuff; let me make it pretty clear what I expect of you: you're supposed to satisfy my needs."

"That's just it, Dakari. It's all about you. I don't know why I was stupid to think that you had it going on. That you really cared about me as a person. I see that's not the case.

You're such an egotistical jerk. You haven't changed at all since last year. You get what you want . . . you're happy. If you don't . . . you move on. Well, move on, brotha, move on. Let me out to my car so I can move on!" I got out and slammed the door. He had some nerve. I detested him.

––––––––––

When I pulled up to my house, the lights were off. That was a good sign. That meant my parents had forgotten about it, and Perry had taken care of it, and everyone was asleep. When I looked down at the clock, I was glad to see the lights were off because it was two in the morning. I had told my parents I was going to spend the night with Rain. And since Dakari's parents were in Columbia, South Carolina, on a business trip, I had left my car at his house around the back, hoping no one would ever know that he and I were off together.

Since it appeared my parents were asleep, I wouldn't have to think about what I would say to them until tomorrow. And tomorrow was the big family vacation. Maybe my parents would forget all about this and I wouldn't have to deal with it at all.

Cool, they didn't put the dead bolt on. Home free! Home free! I thought as I closed the door behind me.

At the same time that I turned around, the lamp in the family room came on. The light was so bright. My dad was sitting there with the belt in his hand. I couldn't believe it, a belt in his hand. Mind you, I'm a high school graduate! My father had a belt in his hand. Surely he didn't think he was going to use that on me. Those days of having a sore behind were over.

"Dad," I said, trying to get on his good side. "I am so sorry about the misunderstanding . . ."

"No misunderstanding, Payton," he cut me off. "You mean

the absolute lie you told me and your mother. Where were you, Payton?"

"I . . . I . . . I was . . ."

"I don't want one more untruth," my dad said in a calm, yet forceful voice.

I could tell by the shortness in his voice that he knew where I had been, but how? I'm sure Miss Pillar figured it out and told them. Though I didn't want to admit the truth, I knew I had to. But surely my dad would never understand. Looking back on the mess I had gotten myself into, I didn't even know what I was thinking. Planning to spend the night with Dakari was way over my head.

"Payton, in a month or two, you're gonna be out of this house on your own, and the decisions you make, you're gonna have to stick with them. There are consequences to trouble. There are consequences to bad decisions. There are consequences to sin. I'm not going to be able to stand at the door waiting for you every night when you get up to Georgia. You are going to have to be responsible for yourself, and the way you're acting now, young lady, I don't know if you're ready. You had your mom all worried. It's two in the morning, and we're supposed to drive at six. You got me all stressed out. I tell you, girl, I'm truly disappointed in you. I actually don't even want to know where you were. Just take your little self on up to your room and go to bed. Get out of my face. I don't wanna deal with you right now."

Actually, I got off easy. He probably would've killed me, had he known I had intended to be in a hotel room with Dakari. Though I hated the secrecy, it was best. I knew I had to keep him from finding out.

———

The next day, I somehow made it to Hilton Head, South Carolina, to vacation with my family. The car ride down in the van wasn't a pleasant one. However, I survived. Pillar's brother didn't end up coming, but her mom and dad were there. It was the first time my father and his brother were going to spend quality time together in years. I hoped that this would turn into a good trip we'd all remember.

Sitting in the beach chair watching my family have a good time, I tried getting the previous night's events out of my head. For some reason, the thoughts just wouldn't leave me. Dakari's actions were too much to bear. However, I couldn't put all the blame on him. I was partly at fault, and that point I'd never get over.

The waters were so peaceful as the waves moved toward me. The sight before my eyes was gentle and intoxicating. I felt peace, even in my uncertainty. Though the night before was a total disaster, I did learn a valuable lesson.

"God," I said as I took in the serene place and humbly talked, "I remember just saying to You yesterday how ready I thought I was. I never even gave consideration to what it says in Your Word. One day I know You'll allow everything to be perfect in that area for me, and I will be able to experience total love in the way in which You created. Now, almost too late, I am so sorry for trying to do things Payton's way and not God's way. Forgive me, Lord, and thanks for giving me a window out. I saw Your light before it was really too late. Thanks for not giving up on me. I love You. In Jesus' name. Amen."

Pillar's parents were no more than six feet away from me. Everyone else was in the ocean, except Grandma. She was back at the beach house preparing lunch. Hilton Head was a beautiful place; vacationers come from all parts of the country.

We were staying at the Palmetto Dunes, and on this particular resort, there was almost everything you'd ever want on a vacation: golf courses, restaurants, hotels, apartments, and beach homes. We came here every summer and now that I was about to go to college, this might be my last summer joining my family here.

Seeing my aunt and uncle, who we very rarely see, have so much fun, made me glad that my parents didn't punish me and make me stay home. They probably wouldn't trust me at home by myself anyway. I was feeling their distance, their disapproval of my actions. However, they didn't leave me out, and for that I was grateful.

"Look at them," I heard a guy say behind me. "That disgusts me. Look at that couple over there. The black guy and the white lady. She ought to know better than wanting to associate herself with such."

"Ugh! I see what you mean," the other man replied. "I don't know what's wrong with some people. Stooping so low, dating outside their race."

"Yeah," the other man agreed. "All this mixing is getting on my nerves. I'm going over and tell them how ridiculous their little affair is. They should keep that filth in their room."

Looking over my shoulder, I was saddened to see two middle-aged white men, full of hate. As the bigger one got up out of his seat to go towards my uncle and his wife, I knew the confrontation wouldn't be a good one. This Hilton Head trip was supposed to be pleasant, but I sensed rough waves ahead. Because of people's prejudice, it wouldn't be smooth sailing. Lately, everything I had planned was going astray. The trip Dakari and I took got all messed up and this family retreat seemed to be turning into a nightmare. My summer was full of strife. I was vacationing with trouble.

8

Dating
Just Because

Without thinking, I leaped from my seat and stood in front of the man who was about to confront my uncle. This man looked eerie. He was three times my size, but not bigger in character, and that's what counted. That was what was going to allow me to say what I needed to say. The man was a jerk, and the thought of straightening him out was most definitely appealing.

That attitude of not judging people because of skin color was going to help me for college. I could no longer rely on my parents to shield me from racism. And though I didn't like what the man was saying, a part of me felt the same way. I used to always hate the fact that my uncle's wife, Margie, was white. Never had a reason, just remembered my grandmother not liking it. Because she didn't like it, I didn't like it either, but that wasn't right.

Who are we to say who is for someone else? As long as we're adhering to what the Word says, it's OK. That's the problem, though. Many don't know God's Word, much less practice it. I should know.

"Yes, can I help you?" the man said, curling his lip, noticing that he couldn't take a step forward since I was in his way.

"I overheard you, sir, and with all due respect, the gentleman to whom you are about to talk to is my uncle, and that's not his girlfriend, OK? That's his wife. We're here on vacation, and we don't want any trouble. And you may have your buddy right there, but my dad is here, and so is my brother and six other men in my family. I don't think you want any trouble either."

"That's his wife?" he said doubtfully. "She's crazy."

"Well, that's your opinion, sir. However, last I checked, this was public property. If you don't like it, then that's your problem. Don't make it my uncle's."

My dad and Uncle Percy noticed me talking with the mean-looking gentleman, and they started coming my way. The man's partner came and pulled him away.

"C'mon. We don't want no trouble. Let's go," the other guy stated.

Immediately they fled the scene. There wasn't a confrontation. I was glad it was avoided.

"What was all that about?" Pillar's dad questioned me.

My aunt Margie said, "Oh, I'm sure it's the same old stuff. Just the same old horrible stuff. We've been married now for twenty years. When is this ever gonna end? When is the bigotry ever gonna end?"

The despair in her voice was disheartening. Though I couldn't feel her pain, I was weighed down with sadness. Though I wasn't at a place where I felt comfortable dating a person of another color, I did know deep down if anyone else wanted to, they shouldn't be persecuted by others.

I wondered when we'd get away from that. When would the world stop being so narrow-minded? I keep hoping that people will be good at heart, and then stuff like this happens. It gets tiring.

The rest of the trip wasn't great either. It rained in Hilton Head, and all of us were cooped up in the house that was extremely big, but not big enough. I say that because, after spending more than forty-eight hours in it with tons of folks, it became smaller and smaller to all of us.

Not only were my parents still mad at me for lying to them, but I was sick. Those two facts made my trip miserable. So tired of being cooped up in the house, one day I just went out. The rain wasn't gonna bother me, and hours later I paid for it. My nose was stuffy, my neck was achy, and my throat was throbbing with pain.

No one said, "I told you so;" they just nursed me our last few days there as well as our first couple of days back home. I wished I would have listened and not been such a hardhead. I wanted to run away from every horrible thought consuming my mind.

The incident with Dakari was too much to handle. Him forcing himself on me. He wasn't the same guy I thought I knew. He surely wasn't the guy I wanted to be with, or have any association with. And how was I to deal with that, knowing that we'd be at the University of Georgia together in a couple of months?

I was now a high school graduate. Back in high school, I had questions with no answers. Surely I thought that once I had finished my days at Lucy Laney, the "no answers" would be no more, but I was wrong. I guess that's what life's all about. Learning day by day, and not taking everything for granted, but getting better with each experience. And sometimes with the tough experiences, I learned valuable lessons.

"Mommm. I think I got strep. My throat is hurting," I said to her, cooped up in my bed.

Pillar and her parents had two more days before leaving for Denver. I was supposed to accompany them. Their gift to me for graduating. Never been to Denver. Never wanted to go to Denver. Maybe this would be a good thing having strep throat after all. I wouldn't have to go.

Before I could rest, I had visitors. Lynzi, Dymond, and Rain had entered into my space. My space that I didn't want to be interrupted. I was just kinda tired. Kinda fed up. Still kinda stressed and strained about the incident with Dakari that I could not discuss. Knowing Rain had blown my cover, I knew she was gon' mention it. But before she went there, I stopped her.

"Hey, y'all, I don't even feel good," I mumbled. "Can't really talk about anything. Y'all should come back another time. I don't wanna get you sick. It's summer. You don't wanna be weighed down with a cold." Go find Pillar and hang out with her."

Though I suggested that, I really didn't mean it. I should have told them to leave, but that would've been rude.

"I sho' don't wanna catch no germs," Lynzi said as she took three steps back to the door. "I have a hot date tonight. I'll be hangin' with Pillar. Your cousin is hooking me up."

"Hookin' you up with who?" I sprung up out of the bed, more alert than before.

"Girl, she's hooking me up with a white guy."

"Quit joking," I said to her.

"No, she's serious," Dymond said. "I told her she better watch out playin' them games. The guy thinks she's white."

"Why does he think that?" I asked, not understanding.

"Yo' cousin told the boy she was," Dy responded.

I teased, "Well, he'll be in for a pretty big surprise when he sees her tonight."

"I know, and I'm sayin' you just shouldn't play with people," Dymond reiterated.

I asked, "Who does Pillar know? She's hooking you up with somebody . . . but, I mean, who are these guys?"

"I don't know. Somebody she said she met down there, wherever y'all just came from," Lynzi replied.

"Hilton Head?" I questioned, shocked.

"Hilton Head. Yeah! She said it was somebody from down there," Lynzi went on. "I thought you would have met the guys."

"I was sick, remember?" I lashed out. "I am pretty much on punishment, thanks to Rain."

Rain defended, "Look, you know you gotta talk directly to folks when you got them covering for ya."

"I left a message on your machine," I told her, somewhat angry.

"Well, you shoulda made sure she got it 'cause she busted you," Dymond joked.

"There's nothing funny about it. Y'all know I almost got a whoopin'."

"What?" Lynzi questioned.

"Girl, I'm serious. My dad tripped. He didn't give me one though, but I am so angry with him. Treating me like I'm five."

Rain pried, "Well, where did you go?"

"See, I don't wanna go there," I muttered, looking the other way.

"Seriously, where did you go? Was it with Dakari? Was it with Tad? Or were you out with a white guy?" Lynzi laughed. Her laughing made me angry. There had been nothing funny about my date. It was a bad experience I was trying to forget.

"Get out. I'm tired. Talk to y'all later," I said in an irritated voice.

They were fed up with me too. As they turned around and left, I heard Lynzi brag about the short halter dress she was gonna wear on her blind date to impress the guy. Her showing off bugged me even more. Maybe on any other day I would have cared that I had ticked them off, but I had too much going on inside of me. So much so that I didn't know where to go to sort it all out, and before I could start to, I had another interruption. The phone.

"Hello," I gasped in a tired voice.

"Payton, hey, lady. It's Shayna. You don't sound like yourself. Everything OK?"

"Other than the fact that I'm sick, my parents are mad at me, I gave up a good guy for an absolute jerk, and I'm faced with going away with a cousin I don't like in a day or so. If you throw all that out the window, then I'm doing pretty good."

Mrs. Mullen suggested, "Well, maybe I'll just call you back when you really are doing good."

"No, I'm sorry," I said to her, trying to shake the anger and get myself together. "How are you? How are you feeling? Are you over the morning sickness? Are you still sick all the time"

"I feel a lot better, thanks. You said something interesting that I'm curious about. You said that you gave up a good guy to go with a jerk. What was all that about? What's going on?"

"I don't know, Shayna. I just made a wrong decision and maybe . . . I don't know . . . I can't even talk about it."

"So you and Tad aren't together anymore? Y'all aren't dating? What's up?"

Part of me was still angry. I didn't know at what, but I was just angry. My first thought was, *Didn't she hear me say that I didn't wanna talk about this?* But I didn't say that; I just swallowed my pride and answered her question.

"No, Shayna. Tad and I aren't together."

"Why not?" she probed.

"Just because. Just because."

"Well, who's the jerk that you were talking about? What's going on? It sounds like you need to talk, and I don't think I'm hanging up the phone until you do."

I broke down and told her the whole story. She was right; I did need someone to talk to, and I was so thankful

God sent her my way. She was so understanding. So caring and concerned for me and all of my issues. So willing to get in the mud and lift me out of depression. It was easy to see how much she wanted to help when I got my pride out of the way.

"So what do I do now? I just can't even seem to sleep. Every time I close my eyes, I just feel Dakari on top of me, and I see myself saying 'No!' and I see him not stopping. I'm just shocked, scared, and hurt. I don't know what to do."

"You gotta pray, Payton. You gotta pray, and I promise you you'll feel better. Also, you may wanna think about telling your parents. If this was really a date rape situation, then you might wanna address it."

"Oh, my gosh! I can't do that. I don't know if it's really that serious. He did stop. It was just one of those weird moments where he didn't, and although it was a few moments, it felt like an hour, or two hours, or forever and he wouldn't stop, but I don't wanna . . . I don't know. I don't think he'll do it to anybody else, and maybe I brought it on myself . . . so I can't tell on him."

"Don't feel like that," she said, cutting me off. "Don't feel like you brought it on yourself."

"Why not? I went out of town with him," I confessed to her.

"Saying, 'No,' means 'No,' Payton! Listen to me now, 'cause I want you to hear this. It doesn't matter when you came to the realization that you didn't wanna go any further with this guy, and though you were wrong to go there, you didn't deserve to have him force himself on you in any way, shape, or form. You gotta believe that for yourself. You gotta feel good that through it all you still did stay strong, and be thankful that he did stop."

She made so much sense. We talked some more, and she listened and she made me feel better. I wasn't completely whole again, but my pieces weren't so scattered. My life wasn't in such shambles. The puzzle of my soul was slowly coming together.

"Payton, please . . . please come get me. You gotta come," the somewhat-strained, familiar voice on the phone said.

I asked, "Lynzi, is that you? I can't tell."

Still a little drowsy from my medicine, I had to make sure it was my friend, 'cause it surely didn't sound like her. And if it was her, it sounded as if something was definitely wrong.

"Yeah, Payton, it's me," the raspy voice said. "You gotta help me, Pay. You gotta help me before he finds me. You gotta help me. Payton, help me!"

I sat up straight in my bed. I knew my friend wasn't kidding. Her demeanor was too on edge. Though she could be a kidder, I knew this time she was serious. Something was very wrong.

"Oh no, Payton! Oh no! I see his lights, Payton! Oh no! I see his lights!"

"Lynzi, tell me what's wrong. You're scaring me. Please tell me what's wrong."

"He's coming after me. He might hurt me worse, Payton. Please help me."

Not knowing what else to do, I clicked over and quickly dialed 911.

"Operator, I cannot make out what's wrong with my friend. I don't think she's acting. She sounds like she's in trouble. I cannot tell where she is. I need help. I need help," I said, terrified.

"Payton, Payton, where did you go? Payton, where did you go?" my panicked friend said to me when I clicked back over.

"I'm right here. I'm right, here Lynzi. Tell me where you

are. Tell me what's wrong."

"He's looking for me. He's looking for me; I know he is. I can tell. Ouch! Payton, I'm hurt."

Chills went up my spine, and I didn't know what to do. Didn't know what to say.

Then the calm voice of the operator said, "Lynzi, where are you?"

"I'm hiding in the bleachers. I'm hiding in the bleachers behind my high school so he can't find me. I'm hiding under the bleachers behind my high school so he can't get me," she repeated.

"Who? So who can't find you?"

"Tom. Thomas Green. He was my blind date. A white guy who was furious to find out his date was black. He was my date and he . . . he . . ."

"Lynzi," the voice of the operator said again, "were you raped?"

"No, he tried," my friend let out in a sigh. "But I was assaulted."

As Lynzi started wailing and wailing and wasn't making much sense, she did manage to give enough information to get cops out to her location. However, the operator wanted me to stay on the line with her to keep her somewhat calm. I wasn't very good.

Though I wasn't physically bruised or beaten, not sharing my experience the week before allowed her to go into her situation with her guard down, and it should have been up. If Dakari, someone I knew, trusted, and loved could freak out in just a minute and be somebody different, surely some guy whom she didn't even know that wasn't really expecting her as his date, could flip out and be domineering and overbearing.

As the operator and I waited on the phone with Lynzi for the police to arrive, I silently started crying within.

"I got away, Payton. I got away. I got away from him.

After he punched me repeatedly, I found the strength to kick the mess out of him. That's when I got away. I ran away, Payton. I ran away from him. He tried to force himself on me, but I got away. I got away."

"I'm glad you got away. Hold on. Hold on, Lynzi. I'm glad you got away," I spoke, trying to ease her fears.

All of a sudden I got even more afraid. Where was my cousin? In all of this and through all of this she had never mentioned Pillar. Though I was afraid to say the words, I knew I had to. No, I didn't want to ask the question, but it needed to come out. Though I didn't want any bad news, I had to know.

"Lynzi, where's Pillar?"

After three brutal seconds of silence, I repeated the question.

"Lynzi where's Pillar?"

"Movies. She's with the other guy at the movies. We didn't wanna see the movie. I should have seen the movie, but we dropped them off and kept going. We gotta get to her. We gotta get to her. She's at the movies."

Lord, thank You, I prayed silently. *Thank You for letting Pillar be OK for the moment. I gotta get to her though, Lord. I gotta get to her before the movie lets out. Help me. Give me the strength. Give me the strength to endure during this trial, a trial I feel is my fault, Lord. I know sometimes an experience we go through is for us to learn and help others, and if only I would've . . . could've . . . should've . . . opened my mouth. Maybe, Lord . . . I can't go back. I can't do this to myself. I can't shake this. Help me, Lord. Help me shake this. I'm losing it.*

Though an actual rape did not occur, Lynzi had wounds that needed to be treated immediately. The police took Lynzi to a rape crisis center where they would question her and get all the necessary information for finding the horrible person who had made her evening a nightmare. I told my mother everything that happened, and of course she told my dad and uncle. They went straight to the movie theater to pick up Pillar.

My mom drove me to see Lynzi, and though I was still physically ill, my ailments weren't at all a concern anymore. My full focus was on my girlfriend and how, in any way, I could ease her pain.

As soon as she saw me come through the door, she reached out her arms for a hug. Both of us started sobbing. I knew why she had tears, and she probably thought I was crying because she was, but my issues were much deeper than that.

Though I was feeling her situation, I was beating myself up within 'cause I felt like I could've stopped it, and I didn't. By opening my mouth, I could've helped, and I didn't. By telling her about my similar incident, I could've prevented hers, but I didn't.

"It'll be OK. Payton, I'll be OK," Lynzi said, trying to be strong. "This is a lot though. This is a lot. 'Cause I didn't like this guy. I didn't know this guy. I guess I was rebelling 'cause of my dad. He's dating a twenty-four-year-old white chick, you know."

I replied, "No, I didn't know that."

"Yeah, well, he is," she continued. "I thought he was gon' get back with my mom, after everything that happened to me. I just knew my folks were gonna start dating again. My dad blows my dream by being attracted to a woman with blond hair and blue eyes. And I don't know, I didn't like it. So I just rebelled. I just went out with this guy for no reason, and I guess this is what I get. I had no good reason for going out with him."

She grasped her aching face. With her puffy jaw and black eye, she hardly looked like the Lynzi I knew. The dress she wore, the hot pink mini halter dress that she bragged about wearing, was ripped in several places.

"Look where it got me," Lynzi voiced as she pointed to herself. "I was dating just because."

9

Mending the Tear

"It's gon' be OK Lynzi, you're right. It's gon' be OK," I told her, trying to give her comfort at the crisis center.

We pulled away from our embrace. I wiped her tears—tears that I hated she had.

My mother came rushing in and said, "Your father just called. He said that Pillar was not at the movies. Lynzi sweetie, where else do you think she could be?"

"Well, she didn't want the guys to come to the house, so we met them in the mall parking lot."

"You met where? And parked where exactly?" my mom questioned to get absolute clarity.

"We parked . . . we parked by Sears, but . . . the movie theater that they went to is on the other side of the mall. So maybe . . . maybe they're walking to the car."

"Perry, honey, did you get that?" my mom said to my dad through the receiver.

The thought of something happening to my cousin scared me. What if she couldn't be found? No! I couldn't let myself give up. Surely, Pillar was OK.

"Pillar! Pillar!" I screamed in the middle of my sleep, afraid she wasn't there. "Pillar!"

The light on the nightstand came on. When I opened my eyes, I was thankful to see Pillar's face. For the first time since she'd been here, sharing my bed didn't seem so bad. I reached out and squeezed her so tight. She hugged back.

"It's OK," she said. "They found me. I know everything. Remember? The guy that assaulted Lynzi is in jail, and nothing happened to me. My date was just fine. You must have been dreaming. Lynzi's gone home now. She's resting with her mom. Things aren't totally OK, but I am. I'm OK."

"Pillar, my last dating experience was crazy. The guy almost forced himself on me. I should have told both you and Lynzi. We can never be too careful. I don't know what I would've done if something had happened to you," I voiced with sincerity.

"Nothing happened to me. I'm OK, but I'm glad you care. And I'm sorry you went through that. I'm also sorry I left your friend alone with that guy. I just never thought . . ."

"I don't blame you," I told her. "I know Lynzi doesn't blame you either. I know this might sound mushy, Pillar, 'cause we've just gone through all this mushy stuff, but I love you, and I'm sorry. I wasn't the best cousin I could be and all that stuff. But now that I see you right here, I wanted to tell you that because I wouldn't want anything to happen to you, and I'd never get to say what's really on my heart and what I do feel."

"Well, I care about you too, Payton, and I've given you lots of reasons not to like me or not to want me around, but when it comes down to it, I do want you to want me around. And I know I'm on my way back to Denver, and things are crazy down here, and you didn't really want to go, but maybe you do need to kinda get away. Maybe it would be good for you to be in a different environment for a while. It would only be a week. Come out and see my life. Let's work on us. Let's be what we should be to each other. Let's be what we can be to each other. Come."

"That sounds really good," I told her as two tears fell from my face. "That sounds real good. I know I'll enjoy getting to know who you are on the inside."

Seems like anytime there's trouble, I always have someone that comes to the forefront of my mind as a good friend. Someone that could put a good perspective on things and encourage me in the darkest hour. That person was Tad Taylor.

I hadn't talked to him for a while, and I had practically kicked him to the curb. Though I didn't need him as a companion, I needed him as a friend. So I reached out. Vulnerably, I reached out. He could have said no. He could have told me he didn't want to see me, but he didn't. His genuine heart helped him move past his pride and agree to see me.

We sat by the small pond out his way. The atmosphere was so serene in South Carolina. Looking around at the peaceful waters and the beautiful sky, I couldn't believe that my life, right now, was so opposite. My life was so unquiet. So upside down. So not perfect. So ugly.

"What's on your mind, Payton? Did you really want to talk to me? You're so quiet. I don't wanna press you, but you really had me worried on the phone. If you changed your mind and you don't want to talk, I understand," Tad said, respecting my feelings.

I was quiet. I didn't say anything. I couldn't respond.

He stood up and said, "Well, maybe we should just go back to my house and you can go home."

I grabbed his arm before he could walk away and said, "No. No, please bear with me, Tad. I do need to talk to you. I need to get this out. I need to talk to someone." Gaining composure, I slowly said, "Lynzi was physically assaulted."

"Ah . . . man, Payton. Are you serious?" he said with concern.

"Yeah, unfortunately, Tad. I'm really serious, and I think it's my fault. Well, no, I know it's my fault. I know I could've prevented it, and..."

"What do you mean you could've prevented it? Why do you always do that? I know you're emotional right now, really sensitive, and I'm not trying to come down on you, but you're always coming down on yourself. It really bugs me. Why do you put so much on yourself in other people's situations? Why do you feel like you can stop some guy from doing something to your friend? I mean, I don't get it," he said, throwing up his hands.

It was going to be so hard to tell him what I was about to say to make him understand that I could've stopped this. I could've prevented Lynzi's horrible situation. But I had no clue of how to tell him of my terrible encounter.

"I don't know why I'm telling you this. Maybe to clear my own conscience. Maybe to feel better. Somehow in all of this stuff I need relief. But . . . it's weird."

"What do you mean, it's weird? All of this is a little hard for me to understand, so talk. Talk. Tell me," he said.

"Well, what I'm trying to say . . ."

"Get to it. Just tell me. I wanna know why you feel this is your fault."

"Because it happened to me a week earlier, OK?" I yelled.

"You mean, you got assaulted?" He stood up, as waves of fear, confusion, and caring crossed his face.

"No! I almost did, though, and I never told anybody. If

I would've told Lynzi about what happened to me, then maybe . . . I know I . . . she wouldn't have been . . . I just . . ."

I was a wreck. I couldn't finish anything. Couldn't say anymore. Nothing else would come out of my mouth except cries of sorrow. I felt like such a horrible person. I had treated Tad so badly, yet he was here. Here listening to me. Here wanting to help me.

When I couldn't speak another word, he grabbed me, pulled me tight in his arms, and said, "It'll be OK."

This guy cared about me deeper than Dakari ever could. If I was smart enough to realize that, smart enough not to miss anything that Dakari wasn't giving, I could've avoided my situation. Hindsight, as they say, is 20/20, but, boy, did I wish I could correct so much, 'cause it felt good, secure, and safe in Tad's arms. Like he wanted nothing but my best. Nothing but a happy Payton Autumn Skky.

I was hurting and mainly because of poor choices. I had brought a lot of things on myself. After about five minutes or so, I calmed down.

"So who was it, Payton? Who was this guy who tried to force himself on you? I wanna know."

Now see? I thought to myself. I was not tryin' to tell him this information so he could go and make it a bigger problem. However, he didn't seem to be letting up. He kept asking and wanted to know.

Though I was flattered that he wanted to fix this for me, he couldn't. And knowing the person's name wasn't going to help anything. The damage was done, and there didn't need to be more pieces to put back together, and in some kind of way, I had to explain this to Tad.

"Why do you keep asking me, Tad? I said I didn't wanna tell you. I said I didn't wanna talk about who it was and all this stuff. Just like that guy who kept going on and on trying to force himself on me, you're now trying to force me to tell you who it is and I don't wanna tell you. OK? No."

"Listen, Payton," he said in frustration, "I respect your position, but if somebody hurt you, I only want to know because I care. Based on how you're trippin', I think I know who it is."

"Don't go speculating, Tad. This is too big a deal to accuse the wrong person. Seriously, just drop it. Please," I asked him, using another tactic. "I just told you all this stuff because I feel so bad."

"Well, you can't do anything about the past, but what you can do is tell your other friends. Make sure they don't fall victim to the same thing you're talking about. I encourage you to share with Lynzi what you're feeling. And, to be honest, though that might have helped her not have the similar thing happen, you can't ever be sure. I mean, Lynzi Crandle I know is very strong-willed. Something is always goin' on with her. I know she's your girl and all, and she's cool. She's so cool, but she's stubborn. And even if you had told her, who's to say that would've had anything to do with what she thought? She thinks she can take care of herself. Like you, she's tough. Sometimes we can't be so hardheaded, you know what I mean? Crazy things happen when we are stubborn. I just want you to start thinking more because I don't want you to regret anything else."

Gosh, he made so much sense. In a weird way, he did make me feel better. He was right though. I did owe it to myself to divulge my bad encounter with my friends.

Later that day, I called Rain and Dymond over. They thought I just wanted to say good-bye 'cause I was going out of town for a while, being that I was going to Denver and all. However, my wanting to spend time with them was much deeper than a simple good-bye.

I needed them to hear my story. I needed them to feel it.

I needed them to know it. I needed them to embrace it as their own so they would not fall victim to similar circumstances.

"Are you serious? That happened to you?" Rain said as she stood up and hugged me.

The hug felt strange. Not because I didn't feel her sincerity in giving me the embrace, but I didn't feel like I deserved it. I still felt like I was partly to blame. The people I talked with when I took Lynzi to the crisis center said that it wasn't my fault. That was still hard to grasp.

Dymond spoke as if she read my mind, "Well, you know it wasn't your fault, right?"

"Yeah, I know, but . . ."

"No buts," Dy cut back in. "It wasn't your fault."

"You don't understand. I went with him. I let him feel like I wanted it. Part of me did want it. That's what's so horrible."

"But you said, 'No,' Payton, and 'No' is 'No,' Guys gotta start understanding that. It just makes me so angry that just because you're batting you eyes and puckering your lips, they assume you're ready to give up everything. That is still not a yes. I'm not trying to let you off the hook or nothing, but we all been there. I mean, you know my story. I went all the way, but it's because I chose to, not because someone decided they wanted it. Regardless of what made him start, don't you be feeling like you brought this on yourself. You didn't, girl. You didn't."

"What are you thinking, Rain?" I questioned my friend.

"I don't know. I guess this makes me respect Tyson so much more because there's so many times when he could've forced himself on me. I gave him lots of reasons to think that I wanted it and got him all excited about it, and I stopped. I'm not saying he was always happy about it, but he never kept going. Gosh . . ."

"I know you guys have boyfriends and stuff, like Fatz

and Tyson, but I don't want my business all out in the streets. I'm telling you guys because this was somebody that I knew; names aren't important, so don't ask me."

"It ain't like we don't know," Dymond stated with certainty.

"Yeah, really. You were supposed to be at my house that night, remember? Just makes sense with the time. Who else would you wanna give it up to? Tad just don't seem like the kinda guy that would force himself on you. So it's gotta be Dakari," Rain rationalized.

"Think whatever you want, but like I said, I'm not confirming any names. It's over. Done with. Whatever. I just don't want it out in the streets. You guys needed to know because if I would've told Lynzi . . ."

"Don't even go there. Girl, you know that ain't the truth. So what if you would've told Lynzi? Lynzi ain't no virgin either. She went out on this date with this guy; she knew what she was gettin' into. Whatever happened with Dakari . . . "

"I didn't mention any names," I cut in and said.

"Yeah, OK. Whatever happened with this guy, who we're not supposed to know who it is, but we know who it is . . . whatever happened with that situation, I don't think it could've prevented what happened to Lynzi."

"Well, even if it couldn't have, it should have been out there. I should've told her, and that's why I'm telling you guys now. It may matter one day. Tyson might be cool as cool for nine months, and on that tenth month he might trip in that area. And you just need to be aware. We can't send wrong signals. I mean, we need to take responsibilities as girls, too. We need to be like 'No!' and know that our 'No' is a 'No,' and not be shaky and not know what we want."

"Yeah, but it's hard when you really care about somebody," Rain said.

"I know it's hard, but we gotta find our strength in Christ. We gotta take His strength and make it our own. Rain, when you go to the Atlanta University Center, Spelman . . . girrrll, there's going to be guys everywhere. Morris, Brown, Clark, Morehouse; I know you in love with Tyson now, but you just wait. It's gon' become harder and harder to resist that kind of temptation. And Dy, don't trip, girl, up there at Howard . . . I ain't ever been that far north. Y'all know I ain't nothin but a southern girl, but I can just imagine Virginia State, Hampton, Norfolk State, Virginia Union, Bowie State, Howard, all those schools around there. You gon' have nothing but college men everywhere. Fine college men at that. I don't know, we ain't gon' have the strength all the time. We're gonna have to find His strength. Just like I had a deep desire to tell you guys this, I gotta tell Lynzi, too."

"Get out, Payton. Get out. I don't wanna hear any of that now. You mean goody-goody Payton had a similar situation. You could've told me but you didn't. Now you come here after the fact. After you could've prevented my situation, you try apologizing. Get out, Payton! Get out!"

I felt horrible inside. Everyone had let me off the hook. Shayna, Tad, Pillar, Dymond, Rain—but Lynzi wasn't going to. The one who got hurt by my silence wasn't going to let me off. Though it would've been easy to be mad at her, I understood her anger. I knew where it was coming from. I felt that way myself.

"Don't throw me out," I said to her as I moved closer.

"Get back. Get out. I'm so serious. I don't wanna hear it. Not listening to none of your explanations. Nothing you have to say is good enough. You're a trip. You are a stone trip. I really don't wanna hear it right now. I'm dealing with a lot of stuff this year. The last thing I can take on is a friend who I think is a big hypocrite, coming here after the fact. Really, I don't wanna say anything to you. Don't make me pick up something and throw it at you. Girl, let's just end whatever we have left. You go your way and let me just rest without you in my face. I'm kinda tired of you. I'm kinda tired of your self-righteous attitude. A goody two-shoes, who isn't good at all. GET OUT! Get out my face."

When I shut her bedroom door, I was full of despair. I cared so much for her, and she made me feel like I only cared about me. I deserved that, but it was so far from the truth. I was trying to make her feel better, and I only made her feel worse. Both she and I were broken and in so much pain.

I could only hope now, as I walked away, that time could make her see things more clearly. Make her understand where I was coming from. Make her see that she was a big part of my life, and that though I made a mistake, I was very sorry. For now, it was out of my hands. It was now up to our heavenly Father, who had the tough job of mending the tear.

10

Longing for Home

"All your friends are white," I said to my cousin after she and I got back from hanging out at the Cherry Creek Mall in Colorado with some of her buddies.

The ranch-style house was so cool. Though it wasn't mine, it truly felt comfortable. My aunt, Pillar's mom, was really going out of her way to make sure I was OK. I hadn't even been there twenty-four hours, and it felt like a place I wanted to be for a long time.

Her friends were more than different. Though they weren't mean, they definitely weren't receptive. That kinda bothered me. I felt like it was a black/white thing. Maybe it was in my mind, maybe it wasn't. That's why I had to ask her. I had to find out. I had to know what kind of friends she really had. Were they the kind that judged people based on skin color, or were they just kinda timid 'cause they didn't know me? I could tell by her posture that she was taken back by this.

"Why does everything have to be a race issue with you?" Pillar attacked.

"It's not. They just looked at me like I was funny. So I'm asking you what's up? True, I don't know your friends, and I can't speak for all people, but I can say I know how to read white people's faces."

"Well, I just need to tell you," Pillar said, "you're reading too much into what my friends were thinking. This time, you're wrong. And before you get all hot under the collar, you better change your attitude toward people you don't know. You need to give them the benefit of the doubt, as opposed to being so judgmental and feeling like they automatically hate you. This isn't slavery days. All white folks aren't out to get you. You're about to go to a school that is mostly white. You're going to be miserable at that humungous university if you don't change your way of thinking."

I hadn't given much thought to going to the University of Georgia. She was right. I probably would hate it. Hate that part of it, that is, if I didn't get rid of some of the baggage I was carrying. Some of the bitterness I was feeling. Some of the rage because of recent circumstances made me wonder if this is how it was back in the slavery days, that my grandparents talk about. All that pain needed to be dropped out of my world so I could move on.

Agreeing with her revelation, I said, "You know, you're right. I'm sorry. I don't know what's wrong with me. It's just hard sometimes seeing . . ."

Pillar cut me off and said, "You know, that's why I'm not really into this Christian stuff. You're supposed to be saved and all, but you have so much hate inside you. Being biracial, I get it from both sides. I'm sick of white sometimes, and I'm sick of black sometimes. I'm caught in the middle, and they say I'm nothing. I'm nobody. I'm part black and part white, and I'm just me. And me is somebody. Payton, you claim to know God and yet you judge just like everyone else. Because people are mean to you, does that mean you're suppose to be mean back?"

"I said you were right, OK? I said you were right."

"Yeah, but you got some issues, cousin, and you need to deal with them. You tell me that I need the Christ that you have. You say I need to believe in the Jesus that you believe in. It doesn't seem like He's doing much for you, so why do I need Him?"

No words could I say. She was speaking some heavy stuff. It was true. I hadn't been living out what I believed. That needed to change. I needed to seek Christ every day. I needed His help to grow more like Him.

I don't know if it was Denver or if I was just paranoid, but most of the places I went with Pillar, I got strange looks. Maybe they're not used to seeing a black girl. Though I know I'm not the only black girl in Denver, maybe they were wondering why Pillar was hanging out with me. I don't know. I don't wanna read too much into things, but the incidents just stick out.

My second day here, my aunt sent Pillar and I to the grocery store. Well, she was getting some of the things, and I was getting the meat. I was in line for some shrimp, and the man took three other customers before me. I don't know what took me so long to say, "Excuse me, I was waiting here," or for the other people not to say, "Wasn't this girl here before me?" but they just kept going in front of me like I could wait. The butcher was white. The customers that went before me were white. And I wasn't white.

When I called it to his attention, he rudely said, "I'll get to you when I get to you."

Needless to say, my aunt did not have shrimp that day. And when I explained the story to my family, they thought I was making too much out of it. That was Monday. On Wednesday when Pillar took me back to the mall, another incident happened. She was looking in one store, and I was looking in another. We said we'd meet up at the store she was in.

I went to the store where she was supposed to be, and I heard the camera zoom in on me. It seemed like everywhere I went, the little hidden camera was following me. After being in the store for about ten minutes waiting for Pillar to show, I was just kinda standing there browsing and passing time, the saleslady approached me as if I were out of place. It was unnerving.

"Excuse me, miss, can I help you with something? Are you interested in any particular item? This store is very expensive."

Rudely I snapped, "Last time I checked, I could look from the time the store opens till the time the store closes. As a customer, that's a part of shopping, correct?"

Then I opened up my wallet and showed her my three credit cards and a wad of cash. Her mouth dropped open. I could see she felt as stupid as her remarks showed her to be.

Hoping she would get the point, I said, "When I do plan on getting something, you see this stuff—this gets it for me. I don't have to just take it."

"Oh, miss, I'm so sorry. We get a lot of people in here like you that just . . . well, not like you, but you know what I'm saying."

All I could say before walking out the store was, "No, ma'am, I don't know what you're saying."

My uncle took the family out to a restaurant on Friday. Well, everyone except Pillar's brother. He seemed to be so busy. I never saw him around, but he was a college man back home for the summer. I understood what it was like to catch up with friends and not to hang around the crib.

Being that my uncle is my dad's brother, they naturally look a lot alike. I look a lot like my dad, so I would look like my uncle. This woman must have assumed that my uncle was my father, and since Pillar looks so much like her brunette mother, they just assumed that it wasn't my uncle's biological child. They also wrongfully assumed that they were two single parents about to mesh two families together.

I heard one lady whisper to her friend, "Ugh! Look at them over there. I can't believe they're gonna mix those families like that. His daughter. Her daughter. Oh! That's gonna be a mess."

I remember the old saying: Sticks and stones may break my bones . . . but at the time those words WERE hurting. My Aunt Margie heard them, and if my uncle didn't, he had to be deaf. Yet, they ignored it, so I did too. But deep down, I wanted to say something. Retaliate. Vent. Go off. Something, but nothing came out. Following their lead, I didn't show my reaction.

This wasn't my world, though; it was a bigger part of the real world. It wasn't what I was used to. So I guess I had been sheltered. Not to say white people aren't in Augusta, Georgia, but the side I live on, the places I go, there are definitely a lot of blacks around. So unusual stares and people giving their harsh opinions in a loud manner are just not tolerated, and I wanted to go back home. Back to that world. The comfort that I felt when I first stepped foot in Pillar's house was no longer around me, and I desperately wanted to leave.

———————

I had one more night at Pillar's house, and it was twelve hours too long.

"I don't know, girl," I said to Rain on the telephone. "Does it sound like I would dream all that stuff up? There are some serious issues going on."

"Taking your word for it, if what you said happened did

happen, then those are racial issues, but, girl, you are about to go to Georgia . . . University of Georgia. You better deal with it. Get ready for a lot more. That's one of the reasons I'm going to an all-black college. I don't think I'm ready to deal with it. But maybe you are. Maybe this is God's way of showing you. Getting you tough. Getting you prepared for what's to come. So that when you get to school all this other stuff won't distract you, and you can focus on what you need to concentrate on and that's gettin' some good grades."

"Oh, you make sense, Rain, but . . . I mean . . . like my aunt, personally, I don't see how she did it. My uncle is not even a Christian, first of all, and I mean second . . ."

"So are you saying your aunt is a Christian?" Rain asked.

"Yeah, she is. She's the only one in this family that is. And it's cool that she is. I'm praying that my Uncle Percy and Mason and Pillar come around. I don't see how she does it. I don't see how she can take it; having white people talk about her like that. About being with a black man, like it's the filthiest thing in the world. She just sits there all composed and together. If you ask me, she acts like she doesn't even hear it. That is no way to live, if you ask me. Can't go nowhere without people looking at you. I feel so sorry for her."

"You don't feel sorry for your uncle?" Rain asked.

"To be honest, no. My Uncle Percy is strong. He doesn't care what other people think, and I can tell that my aunt does. So, I kinda feel sorry for her because of it. I just . . ."

In the middle of my thoughts, I looked up at the door. My aunt was standing there. She had tears dripping down her face.

"Rain, I'll . . . I'll call you back. Well, you know what? I'll just see you tomorrow. OK, bye."

I turned to my aunt. "Aunt Margie, I didn't see you standing there. How . . . how long . . . how long . . ?"

"Long enough," she replied. "Payton dear, you don't have

to feel sorry for me. I chose my life for myself, and I knew it wasn't going to be easy."

"Some of the situations I've seen you go through are more than uneasy; they're unbearable. You almost break. It's not even me, and I almost break. I'm sorry to say that I feel bad for you, but, Auntie, it's the truth. I hate that you have to go through that, and I don't understand why."

"Why what? Why I put up with this? Why I don't say anything? Why I got married to a black man in the first place, like your grandmother always wonders? Why my parents wondered way back, and people are still wondering 'til this day?"

"I don't know, all of the above," I said honestly.

She came to the side of the bed and grabbed my hand. This was hard for her yet, and I wanted to understand her struggle.

"You know, Payton, it's not like I wanted to make life tough for me and my children. Like I wanted to marry a black man. That wasn't the way it was at all. Your uncle, tough as he may be, told me before I said, 'I do,' that it was not going to be easy. He painted a picture that wasn't a pretty one, and yet my love for him was so strong that the only thing I could do was say, 'I do.' It was natural. As natural as if it were two people of the same race marrying each other. He was it for me. I believed it back then and I still believe it now. And though some people don't understand it, I pray that one day they will. I pray that one day we're all in one accord, one spirit, one heart. Pillar mentioned that you're struggling with some race issues. I know you told me some of the stuff that happened to you here, and maybe I dismissed it too quickly because I was looking for the good in the situation and hoping it was not as bad as you thought. And maybe I was wrong for dismissing it. Maybe I should have addressed it. Because you might have been right, but a lot of things get stirred up sometimes because the other party just feels like it's wrong, and it's not wrong . . ."

"Yeah, Pillar and I talked," I interrupted my aunt. "Boy, she told me that sometimes I just read some things wrong, and maybe that's the case, Aunt Margie, but I just don't think so. Over the last several weeks, so many things have happened to dear friends of mine that were by white people. My ex-boyfriend got forced on the ground by a redneck cop, and my girlfriend got assaulted by a troubled white teen; because of that, plus my experience here, it's a lot of anger and stuff inside of me. I know I want to get rid of it. I don't wanna carry this stuff around and feel the way I do. I'm about to go to a major university where I'm probably gonna be the only black in at least one of my classes. And if I walk into that situation carrying the load I'm carrying now, dealing with racism, I'm probably gonna flunk out of school. My friend, Rain, who I was just talking to, pointed out I'm gonna be too distracted to concentrate on my schoolwork. I'm gonna be trying to work harder than the next person so that they don't think that the black girl is the dumb girl. I don't know, maybe this sounds crazy."

"You know, Payton, I'm not black. But my husband is, and my children, although they are also mine, are viewed as black. Even Pillar, as white as her skin is, is viewed as black because of who her father is. So I know their issues. The only thing I can say to you is, you have to deal with people one at a time. If you come across a white person who doesn't like you because of what you look like, then you gotta deal with that person on their level, and win them over with your heart. If you won't give a person a chance just because you think they're biased against you, without even getting to know them first, then you have to change your heart. Everyone is not the same. You won't even like all black people. You and some of your friends, you guys are pretty different."

I giggled when she said that. I thought about how different

the four of us really were. She couldn't have been more right.

"Yeah, we're definitely all over the map," I chuckled.

"Well, there you go. I've learned to avoid reacting to people who are rude to me and judge me when they don't know my situation. I just think about how Jesus was persecuted and died for my sins, and how I will be with Him one day in heaven, and how He left me His Holy Spirit to be with me daily. So the home that I long for, the home that I want everyone to aspire to have, the home that I hope my husband and children will one day live in, is the home inside me now."

I was perplexed by her statement. I replayed her words in my mind. The puzzled look I gave her let her know that I was confused.

She continued, "I know you're a Christian too, sweetie, which means heaven is also in you. So when you're in a place that's unfamiliar and you don't like it, when you're in a situation that's not really favorable, don't try to flee. Think about what God would do. Think about how you can honor Him in that situation. I know you're going home tomorrow, and I know this hasn't been the best trip, but anytime you wanna talk about issues when you get to college and things get kinda weird, I am white, but I'm also your aunt, and I'd love to be here for you to help you understand people of another culture. Call anytime."

She gripped my hand tight and walked out the door. Her hands reinforced her words. She made so much sense, it was like God sent her for this time. He sent Auntie Margie to talk to me and tell me the truth. It's not other people that control my attitude, but it's the Christ that's in me that gives me wild joy, a smile, sweet laughter. In every situation, I need to find happiness within, and that now took on a different meaning for me. It wasn't simply being back in Augusta, Georgia, but it was seeking God's peace in everything that now symbolized my longing for home.

11

Outside
the Boxes

$\mathcal{B}$eing back home in my own bed felt so good. I missed my own space with my life, my walls, my rules. Being with my extended family in Denver did prove to be a good experience in the end, however. So I was thankful that I went.

The lessons that I learned there I'll carry with me always, both bad and good. I learned that though I was used to things being a certain way, they didn't have to be that way for everything to be OK. And though things might not always go the way I want them to, that's OK too. Knowing that I can accept things better and deal with defeat actually makes me a winner in the long run. That is the ultimate goal.

I felt like I had been saved from depression. Well, maybe the negative experiences coupled with the wonderful talk with my aunt saved me. Going to Denver had somehow revived me and made me appreciate things in a whole other light.

Regardless of what others say, do, or feel around me, I've got to be OK with me. I've got to be able to put on a smiling face and see each day as a good one. When problems arise, I need to be creative enough to not let the challenge of the obstacle get me down. I must find a way to climb over it, move it aside, or simply bust through it.

Since I had been out of touch for a while, I figured I would get in touch with my friends.

I dialed up Tad and said, "Hey, guy. How are you?"

"Payton, you're back. I'm good. How are you?"

"I'm great!"

"Wow! You sound mighty happy. What's up?" he asked.

"I don't know. I guess I'm tired of being down. It's supposed to be the best time of my life. The summer before I go to college, you know, and here I am being weighed down as if my life is over, when it's really just beginning."

"So you got all the answers now," he cut in.

"Umm . . ." I hesitated. "I don't know if I have the answers, but I'm just trying to deal with not having the answers and being cool with that. And appreciating learning the answers as I go along. I don't know, just enjoying life, period. It's such a blessing. I've been thinking about those four girls in that car accident lately."

"You mean the ones that died from Jackson a few months back."

"Yeah. They were from that private school. I just keep thinking that it could've been me. And that . . . God spared me for a reason. He's got something for me, and I need to be happy about doing His will. There's a lot to be done, and He can't use me if I'm not the best I can be."

"What do you think He's got for you to do?"

"Well, I know we're supposed to win souls."

"Yeah," Tad said. "How do you plan on doing that?"

"Like I said, I don't have the answers. It's not like I'm gonna go witnessing in the streets."

"That's not a bad idea," Tad boldly pronounced.

"True. True, but that's not me either, yet," I cautioned.

"So I just wanna appreciate who I am and where I am, and be the best person and Christian I can be, so that when the opportunity presents itself and I have a chance to share the gospel, then I'm ready. If I'm not even happy with me, how can I tell somebody they need Jesus? I gotta get right for Him first. You know what I'm sayin?"

"I hear ya. It sounds cool. That sounds good, Pay," Tad agreed.

Tad and I finished our conversation. It was so refreshing to talk to him about Christ and not about our relationship. Next I called Dymond.

"Girl, it's been so boring around here since you been gone."

"Quit making me feel good," I told her. "What's up, girl?"

"Nothin'. Nothin' too much. Just gettin' my stuff together to go up to D.C. I wanna be ready. Can't forget nothin'. Tryin' to pack it all."

"I heard that," I interjected. "I had a chance to talk to Rain. I know she's going to visit her grandmother."

"Yeah, she left this morning. She said that she was leaving out the day you were coming in."

"What about Lynzi? Did you talk to her?"

"Yeah, but let's not talk about Lynzi," Dymond uttered.

"Why? What's up?"

"Let's not go into that. You seem so happy. I don't want to spoil it."

"Girl, what are you talking about?" I said after she was starting to irritate me. "Just say what's up. What are you talking about?"

"She's still mad at you, OK. Doesn't wanna talk to you. Blames what happened to her on you. All that stuff. Tried to talk her out of thinking that way, but that's the way she feels right now. I don't know. She's just trippin'."

"I understand. That's cool."

"What? What did you say?" Dymond played as if she

didn't hear my reaction.

"I said I understand. I'm praying about the situation. I do take some of the blame. I'm not saying she's crazy to feel that way. I even told you guys that I feel the way she feels. Remember?"

"Yeah, I remember, but that is crazy. You shouldn't feel that way."

"I appreciate you saying that, but sometimes time has to heal it. God has to work with that. I'm OK with not being able to fix it."

"You? Miss 'Have to have all your ducks in a row,' and Miss 'Everybody gotta like you,' are OK with things not being OK?"

I took a deep breath, lay back on my bed, looked toward heaven, and smiled. I was really OK with it, and that felt good. Yeah, I was sad on the inside. Don't get me wrong about Lynzi still being ticked with me, but she has a right to feel like she feels. She went through something even deeper than what I experienced. I knew the side effects would be devastating. So I respected her position at the time.

"I just hope she comes around. I hope it's soon, but I'll give her space until she's ready to forgive me."

"Forgive you? That's a bunch of bull. You being too nice about it. Nobody told Lynzi to be all adventurous and flirt with somebody she didn't know," Dy interjected, having my back.

"You can look back and judge. I don't wanna do that because I'm not perfect either. I've always been so judgmental and so hard on my friends, and I'm just trying to be better. Trying to be a better person. Trying to go to college a little bit more mature than I was my senior year in high school. Don't get me wrong, Dy; I'm going to miss you a lot. I'm even gonna miss some of the things we went through. High school's over, though. We got our diplomas. We're on to bigger things. I gotta handle myself better. I got to handle stress better. Can't let it freak me out when things get messed up."

"Well, me and Fatz broke up. I'm stressed out, bummed out, mad, and upset about it. I wish you could help me," my girlfriend whined.

She went on to tell me that they had irreconcilable differences and didn't want to get into it just then. She'd tell me more later. I didn't push her. Not wanting to talk about it was OK with me. This new attitude of mine was suiting me just fine. Whatever way, whichever way, I was cool with it.

Before I could call Shayna, my mom walked in my room.

"Your dad's downstairs, sweetie. He needs to talk to us."

"Okay, I'll be there in a minute," I said to her to imply I needed a little privacy.

"No, hon, I mean now. You can make your calls later. This seems to be important. Your dad called me before he got home and said he needed to see us. So now, please."

I felt myself reverting back to my old thoughts, so I had to shake it.

"OK, Mom. Sure," I said, hanging up the phone before I could use it.

Fifteen minutes later, my dad stood before us with a big smile plastered across his face. He was so happy, yet I couldn't figure out about what. Last time I was with him, he was pretty upset with me about my sneaking off and all. Maybe he missed me so much that he realized in my absence that I was a pretty good daughter after all. Yeah, I was certain that's what he was going to say to me.

Dad bragged, "Well, we won another trip. Finally! This will be our second Chrysler dealer's trip."

My mom was so happy. I remember seven years ago when my dad went on his first one. It had been his first year taking over his dad's business, and he was a success. The trip had been a gift for fifty of the top dealers in the country who had had the best sales in a certain period. We had gone to San Francisco.

Though I was young, I remember it completely. It was first class all the way. They even had activities for the kids. Though it was nice, I just felt ostracized by the others there. My family was the only black family, and wherever we went, it seemed eyes followed. There were quite a few kids my age, but if it weren't for my brother, I wouldn't have had anyone to hang out with.

"Dad, that's great," I said to him. "But I better pass."

As soon as I said those words, everything stopped. I began thinking: *So what if it was like that seven years ago? You're all grown up, and if nobody talks to you, if you're on the outside, just deal with it. The whole experience would not only make your dad happy, it could also be beneficial. After all, this is one of the last things you can do with your family to make your Dad happy before you go to college. And who knows? It might even be fun. Try it.*

Before my dad could tear into me for not wanting to be there, and my mom could say I had to go, and my brother could try to get out of going 'cause if I wasn't going he wasn't going, I said, "You know what? I changed my mind. I'd love to go, Dad. When do we leave?"

All three of them looked at me with their jaws practically on the ground. Two days later was when the ship sailed to the Bahamas. We'd have to fly out of Atlanta to the port.

"Well, I better unpack and pack again. I'm proud of you, Dad. That's great," I kissed my dad on the cheek and said.

Later that night, I saw him and said, "Dad, I really am proud of you. Ever since you won the first trip, it seems like every quarter you're a little bummed out that you didn't win the contest. I guess I kinda wanted to ask how did you do it this time? What allowed you to be better than you've been? How did you motivate all those salesmen to sell all those cars?"

He gave me a hug and said, "I'm really happy that you're interested. It makes me feel real good that you care, Payton. You haven't been working at the dealership lately, but nothing too much around there has changed. I've just been doing a lot more motivational speeches with the guys in the morning. Trying to make them feel good about who they are. Wanting them to believe that if they feel good about themselves, they could make the customer feel good about buying the product. Before they know it, the number they have envisioned selling is no longer a dream. It's reality. I just get them to veer from the norm, so to speak. And it worked. However, I can't say I'm surprised. I'm very happy. It worked."

I was glad we shared a father-and-daughter moment. My dad's smile showed me he was thrilled, too. We hugged, and it was special.

"Sorry, I gave you a hard time, Daddy."

"You know, I believe you are, Payton. I believe you are."

The first night of the cruise, there was a big reception dinner. All of the families were there, fifty families plus some of the top Chrysler executives and their families. To my surprise, there was one other family that looked like mine. Unfortunately, they seemed to be my grandparents' age, so no other kids were there for me to hang out with. As I slowly glanced around the room, a second time, looking for something other than what was common, I saw lots of young people around Perry Jr and my ages.

Out of fifty families, the only one who got singled out for recognition was the family dealership who was number one in sales, and not just for this quarter, but for the last five years.

This football player, Jett Phillips, was the son. He got most of the attention that day. He was a junior at the University of Florida and as fine as he could be. Blond hair, blue eyes, and a six-one frame. Though he wasn't my type, I had to admit he was *fine.*

Even though I was going to be in the SEC, Southeastern Conference, football wasn't a big deal to me. My brother and my dad were fascinated though. Everyone practically knew who he was except me and my mom. She cared less than I did.

"He's Florida's quarterback. He's up for the Heisman, and he might come out this year as good as he is," Perry leaned over and said to me as Jett stood up and waved to the crowd.

"That boy's got one heck of an arm," my dad said to my mom.

We were here to celebrate selling cars, not a football player. I almost got annoyed with the detour, but then I thought, *There's nothing wrong with being proud.*

After dinner, several of the girls were talking to Jett. I saw him glance at me. He cut a sweet smile my way. I kept walking. I just didn't feel he was smiling at me. He had to be smiling at somebody behind me. I just knew I mistook the direction of his glance. The thought of him being friendly to Payton Skky was just incomprehensible.

Two days later, I was up on the deck relaxing in the sun, taking in hearing the waves around me and relaxing with the movement of the ship.

"Is this seat taken?" I heard a voice gently ask.

When I looked up, I did a double take. It was Jett Phillips asking to sit by me. There were so many available seats beside a whole lot of other girls that were eyeing him up and down. I wasn't planning to give him the time of day, so I didn't know why he would want to sit by me.

"You could sit there if you want. Nobody's sitting there."

"Jett Phillips." He stuck his hand out toward mine. "And you?"

"I'm Payton Skky," I replied, as I held out my hand.

I quickly took my hand away and leaned back down to relax, yet he kept talking to me. He actually wanted to carry on a real conversation. After letting my guard down, I found out that Jett was cool. We connected on so many different levels. And though I thought we were worlds apart, just because he was who he was and I am who I am, I found out that even in those circumstances, the worlds can connect, and it's not such a bad thing.

The two of us were having such a good time that I didn't even notice the time. When I had sat down earlier that day it was eleven o' clock. When I looked at the clock on the deck again it was now four in the afternoon. There was a big bash planned at five o' clock. After swimming in the pool, I had to do my hair, and that in itself was a thirty-minute job.

"I got to go get ready for tonight," I said to him.

"Ahhh, it's just four. We got a whole hour."

"It's gonna take me that to get ready. I gotta wash my hair."

"Just blow-dry it and go, right?"

"No. My hair is totally different from yours," I informed him. "But I'm enjoying myself with you. Enjoying myself more than I ever thought I could."

He grabbed my hand and said, "Well, I've been enjoying myself too, Payton. Will I see you tonight?"

"Yeah," I nodded my head and said, "Tonight."

"Hi!" Jett came right up to me in front of my parents and everyone.

"Hi, Jett. This is my dad and my mom, Mr. and Mrs.

Skky. My brother, Perry. You guys, this is Jett Phillips . . ."

"Jett Phillips," my brother cut me off and said. "I know who he is. Hey, man. What's up? What's up? You got an arm, man. I'm a wide receiver. Thinking about Florida. Who knows, someday you might be throwing to me."

"Looks like you're still in high school."

"Yeah, I was just joking, man," my brother said. "I'm still in high school. Two more years. You'd be done by then . . . with college ball, that is."

"Who knows? Maybe we can hook up on the highest level," Jett said. "I'm sure you have talent."

"Tryin' to be all that. I can ball a little," my brother said. "Tryin' to be as good as you."

Jett said, "Ahh, thanks. I appreciate the confidence. I'm not good. I just got good people on my team, and I know how to hang with them."

"You're being modest," my dad said. "It's good to meet you. Love watching you play, and we wish you much success with the Heisman."

"Thank you, sir. Sir, would you mind if I borrowed Payton for a second?" Jett politely asked.

"Oh, no. No, you guys go right ahead. Y'all have a good time," my dad told Jett, somewhat shocked that he wanted to hang out with me.

We got a lot of looks as we exited out of the dining area. He took me out to the pool where we'd talked earlier that day. It was really fun just hanging out with him. We had our feet dangling in the water.

"What? You're thinking something," he said to me.

Though he didn't know me well, he was right. I was thinking about something. Thoughts of going to Georgia were still scaring me.

"What? What are you thinking? Tell me," he pried, out of concern.

"I'm going to the University of Georgia."

111

"Oh, wrong choice. Don't say anything else. Bad school," he joked. "No, go ahead."

"Well, I'm going to the University of Georgia and I'm black."

"And?" he said.

"Well . . . I just hope I fit in. At my high school, everybody was like me. I'll be going to a place where I'm not like everybody. Get it?"

"Well, I'll tell you right now, you'll have a mixture of people at UGA. You'll have some rednecks. You're gonna have some people that are white that will try to act like they're black. You'll come across everything. You're going to college. You'll find your friends. You'll make your way. Then you'll have some people like me that see a pretty girl and will want to talk to her just because. It won't matter what color she is," Jett proclaimed with wisdom.

"Do you do this all the time?"

"Do what?" he asked.

"Talk to black girls and make them blush."

"Umm, no," he said. "But it's something about you, Payton, that just kind of caught my eye. I've been talking to you all day. You have big dreams, a good head on your shoulders..."

Though I heard what he said, and it was so easy to listen to, it just didn't seem like reality. I bowed my head as sadness fell on me.

"Payton," he said as he took his hand and lifted my chin. "College is going to be what you make of it. Just because you're used to a school with one type of people doesn't mean that where you're going is going to be bad. It's kind of like me with football. Before I played college ball, I had to play high school ball, and I was terrible, a second stringer. I was smaller physically and in heart. I started developing my muscles and working on my thinking, so that I could be all that I wanted to be. My desire needed to meet my expectations. People say I'm a pretty good quarterback now. You know, I'm a Christian and I believe by God's grace I'm good, but when I go out on each Saturday to play, I know Christ is going with me. I don't think like the world says I'm supposed to think anymore and believe the hype about who's gonna lose before we even play a game. I believe that I'm victorious because Christ lives in me, whether the score at the end of the day says my team won or not."

"I'm a Christian too," I smiled and said to him.

"Well, then, you should have that same hope and that same way of thinking. You too should believe that your experiences will be great. Our God wouldn't have it any other way."

"Yeah," I said and hugged him.

The friendship between Jett and I felt so natural. Some of the fears and the ill feelings I had toward another race were slowly disappearing. I had this experience with Jett for a reason. God wanted me to see that every person, as my auntie told me back in Denver, isn't the same. Jett was special, not just because he was a great quarterback or because he was a blond-headed white guy. He was special because he had a way of making other people he met feel special.

Life for me was getting better. I fully understood my new perspective. In Christ Jesus, I am a conqueror. No weapon formed against me can prosper. I felt great and I didn't believe the hype that all people are one way, or that because of who I am, I can't be anything. That was not true; because of who I am and Who lives in me, I can be anything. I was thinking above the norm. I was thinking better than I ever had. I was thinking outside boxes.

12

Picking People Up

$\mathcal{B}$eing in Jett Phillips's arms brought such comfort. In him I had found a new friend. God allowed this gentleman to come into my life to teach me a valuable lesson. One that I'd always remember. Jett Phillips came into my life and embraced me as his friend to show me that no matter how different people are, if they try, they can find a common thread that will give them an intimate bond.

"You're a pretty good dancer," he said softly in my ear.

"I think I should be saying that to you," I teased.

"Ohh, what are you trying to say? That we can't jump and we don't have any rhythm? More myths that aren't true about all of us," he laughed at me.

The openness we'd shared was so deep. It was hard to describe the feelings I had for him. Though I hadn't known him long, I knew I cared about the handsome man before me. Tonight was the last night I'd see him for who knew how long. The next day I'd be heading back to Augusta, Georgia, getting ready for school, and Jett would leave here and go immediately to the University of Florida and start football camp.

"Have I told you you look beautiful tonight?"

"Yes," I laughed. "I think that's the fourth time you've said that, but thank you. It makes me feel good each and every time you say it," I blushed.

"Well, then, let me say it again. You look beautiful tonight. Purple is your color."

The purple, short formal dress was a graduation present from my mom. I didn't think I was going to have anyplace to wear it, but when I reviewed the itinerary for this trip and I saw the attire for the final dinner was semi-formal, I got excited because I was going to get to wear my dress, never knowing that a nice gentleman would get to appreciate it. When I bought it, I thought I was only wearing it for me and, oh, was I so glad I was wrong! I was so glad I had been wrong about many things.

We talked on deck later that evening in the moonlight. He shared his fantasies and fears. I listened intently.

"You know, Payton Skky, I'm glad I met you. Football is my whole life, and when I first got on this ship I had a new bunch of fans in addition to the ones I already have. You can get tired of fans . . . and you were what I needed. I needed a friend."

"Well, you don't have to thank me," I told him as my eyes met his. "Not being so closed-minded has given me a new perspective to see things a different way. I thought I was out of school for the summer at least, but you taught me a good lesson. I now value your friendship too, Jett Phillips. So on the lighter side of things, how many touchdown passes are you going to throw this year? Are you going to win the Heisman as a junior or what? You can only have two interceptions the whole season. You know that, right?"

The smile on his face turned to a grim stare. He moved away from me and leaned over the rail. The blue seas were peaceful, but the thoughts going on with my buddy were anything but.

"You've talked to me; you've helped me see some things. What's going on, Jett? What's up?" I asked with a serious concern.

"There's so much pressure on me. I don't know if I can live up to it. My dad is so into me going pro. He's thinking we can buy more dealerships if I get a big NFL contract. My coach is so into me winning the Heisman. That will secure his job for him. All the fellas on the team expect me to carry them to the national championship. It's just a lot. It's just a lot. What happens if I don't live up to the expectations?" He threw up his hands and tried to walk away.

I grabbed his arm. I knew I had to encourage him. He didn't need to carry such a heavy load. I felt the weight of his burden. For a split second I tried putting myself in his shoes, and I saw how difficult it was going to be to walk in them. Yet my friend couldn't stay dejected. The battle before him was going to be a tough one. He had to be prepared for it. Not prepared to win, but prepared to fight. I was with him at that moment to give him the encouragement to charge on.

"Just go out there and do your best. God's best. Make Him proud. Please Him. Seek the applause of heaven and not the applause of a stadium full of fans. I promise you whatever happens, Jett Phillips, it will be OK."

With the wind blowing across my face, this humble athlete gave me a peck on the cheek. I was finally seeing the bigger picture. Learning what's really important in life. Understanding things that count, and with the gesture that Jett made, I knew what I said to him was just what he needed to let the fear inside him go free.

God calls us as Christians to be our brother's keeper, and that means assuming the burdens of another as if they were your own. Not just the burdens of people who are physically like you, but people who are like you in spirit.

"I'll miss you," I said to him.

He teased, "Don't worry. You'll see me when we beat Georgia."

We both laughed. *Thank You, Lord,* I thought inside, *for allowing me to meet this guy. You always know what I need, Father, and I love You.*

"So how was your grandmother?" I said to Rain over the phone a few days later.

"I had a good time with Nanna. It's so weird. She's getting old and frail. I remember when she used to take me horseback riding and now she can barely walk. My mother's mother passed away when I was three, so I never really knew her, but I've been close to my dad's mom all my life, Payton. I hate having to watch my grandmother deteriorate before my eyes."

"I'm so sorry to hear that," I said with compassion.

"I don't need you to feel sorry for me or anything. Nanna's not dying. It's just tough."

"Well, I'm glad you were able to spend some time with her. I'm sure it made her feel good seeing you. Even though it was hard, you probably made her summer. And if you think about that, it was worth being uncomfortable, don't you think?"

"Yeah, she smiled and hugged me so tight before I left. Payton, she didn't even want to let me go. It was definitely a moving experience. She told me she was proud of me, and she remembered her Spelman days. It was kind of neat hearing some of her stories. You're right; I am glad I went. Thanks."

"So, you talked to anybody?" I asked, changing the subject.

"Yeah, I saw Lynzi. Her face is healed, but she still has nightmares. You need to go and talk to her. She said she's still joining the army."

"Well, I knew she was going to put off school for a minute, but is the army right?"

"Yeah, she said she needs some discipline. She's serious about it too. She took a physical and went through the first steps. She's serious about it."

After I talked to Rain, I worked up the nerve to call Lynzi. It took awhile, but finally after doing some chores, I reluctantly phoned. With the caller I.D., I'm sure seeing my number she decided not to pick up the phone, 'cause Rain told me she just talked to her and she wouldn't be going out all day. So Lynzi couldn't have gone anywhere or been in the shower or anything like that. I know Lynzi; if she doesn't want to talk to anybody she avoids them, and it just so happened that she was avoiding me.

I was so fed up with her being a baby about the whole situation. I grabbed my keys and my purse and headed to her house. I knew she was mad and everything, but she was going to talk to me. She had some nerve dragging this whole thing out. I said I understood and I did, but this was just ridiculous.

"Lynzi is trippin' and we're gonna talk about it," I said out loud to myself in the car.

When I rung the doorbell I stepped away from the peephole so she couldn't see my face. Her mother's car wasn't there, but hers was, so I knew that we'd have time to talk through our differences.

"So who is it?" she said rudely. "You don't answer; you don't come in. I'm serious. You better say something."

"Lynzi, it's me," I said in a sweet tone. There was silence

from the other side of the steel door.

"Payton, I have nothing to say to you. Nothing to say to you," she said slowly. "Leave."

I just kept ringing the doorbell over and over and over and over. I figured she would get tired sooner or later and open the door. Finally after about twenty rings my theory worked and the maroon door opened. The screeching sound the door made mirrored the discomfort that my heart felt.

Although I wanted to talk to Lynzi desperately, I just didn't know quite what to say. I practiced my lines in the car and I was angry. That changed when I saw my weary-looking friend open the door. It appeared as if she hadn't eaten, taken a bath, or done anything for days.

"Payton, whatever you have to say, I don't want to hear it. Please go," Lynzi voiced before she started shutting the door.

I put my foot in the way.

"Lynzi, I feel your . . ."

She cut me off, opened the door, stood right in my face, and said, "Don't even try to say you feel or understand or know what I'm going through. You have no clue what it feels like to be physically violated, or to take twenty showers and still feel dirtier than you've ever felt in your entire life. Even though he didn't go all the way, it feels like he destroyed me. You have no clue how miserable it is to wake up in the middle of the night in cold sweats, feeling so fed up, like you can't even breathe, as if you're being choked by some stranger whose face can't ever leave your mind."

She was right. I didn't know what it felt like to be in her position. Since I'd been going through so much stuff on my own, I hadn't even thought of her daily struggles, and how these past events had been affecting her. I was going to walk away because she was right, but then I thought about it, just before the door slammed shut, that she wasn't right, not completely anyway.

"Lynzi!" I stood my ground. "I'm torn up not because my experience was your experience, or not even because it came close to what happened to you, but I feel it because you're going through it, and though it's not to the same degree, it's bad enough. I can't feel good about too much knowing that my good friend is in pain. Your problem is my problem; don't you get it? I share your burden and I want to do something to lift it."

"A little too late, Payton. A little too late," my former friend pronounced. "Sounds good. Sounds sobby. Sounds sweet, but I'm really not in the mood to hear it. So go to college. Go your merry way, and leave me alone."

I was so taken back that she was still being mean that I wasn't prepared for the slam that was next to come. It was so loud, and yet, there was nothing I could do. I had said all there was to say, and she wasn't interested in hearing it.

"Father," I prayed as I walked to my car, "I don't know what else to do. I am sorry for my part in Lynzi's dilemma, but it's time for healing, and I feel that because I think You placed it in my heart to get her through it, but she won't budge. I'm trying not to be angry. Just help her. Please help her."

When I called over to Tad's house, his mother told me that he had gone fishing by himself, and lately he had been in a depressed state. Mrs. Taylor told me that Tad was finally dealing with the death of his grandmother. He had been so strong for his family for so long that it had finally affected him, and he was shutting everyone out. She gave me the directions to the pond, and I headed up there.

"Can a friend join you?" I said to him as I watched him throw pebbles into the water.

"Not much company, Payton, but it's good to see you.

How you been?"

He didn't get up, so I went over and hugged the back of his neck, and sat down beside him.

"I thought you were supposed to be fishing. Where's the fish?"

"I didn't really feel like it," he muttered.

"I thought you were supposed to be at football camp. I called your mom to get your phone number up there," I questioned. "I was surprised to find you were still here."

"No, actually, we report in the morning, but I'm thinking of not going. I'm tired of football. I need to get an education. Football is just a diversion. I don't know if I want to play anymore."

"Okay, guy." I emptied his hands of the rocks and held both of them in mine. "What's really going on?"

Tad didn't say anything. He just had a blank stare towards the sky. All of a sudden, he became overcome with emotion. When tears trickled down his face about the same time he broke down, so tired of carrying his baggage, he just wanted to drop it. The sky that he was staring at so intensely turned from bright red to gray. Then droplets of rain started falling on the two of us. I just held Tad in my arms, and he sobbed and I sobbed.

The rain fell harder on the two of us. Probably the first time in my life I didn't care about my hair getting messed up. It was more important just to be there for him. I had to waddle in the mud—the mud of the rain and the mud of his distress.

After a few minutes we moved over to a tree, and I said, "I know you miss her, but it's good to feel it. It's OK to show what's inside. It's OK, but giving up the things you're good at, your grandmother would never want that."

"Well, if I hadn't been playing ball in the first place, I would have been able to spend more time with her. I would have been there for her in her last days. Even after the football season, almost every weekend I was gone. Going on recruiting trips and concentrating so much on me that I didn't even see she was suffering. What kind of grandson was I, you know? I refuse to let it happen again. I refuse to be so into what's going on with me, that I can't be there for the folks that I care about."

"But the folks that you care about are glad that you have something positive in your life. So many guys your age are dead, in jail, into drugs, or who knows what else? Everybody always says it; we can't deny it, and it's mostly true. Look at you—you have a full scholarship to a major university and you're good at something positive. You have the opportunity to get a great education and go on to really make your family proud. Don't walk away from that. Don't you think your grandmother wasn't proud because you were doing it? I know if she were here, she would want you to continue for her. For her, Tad, you've got to continue."

All of a sudden he changed tones with me and went from upset to absolutely angry. "You don't know what you're talking about, Payton. You don't know. There were so many things about my grandmother that I never even got a chance to ask, and I'll never be able to ask. She's gone, OK? I'll never get that time back. Football did it, me being so into me."

"What are you talking about? Explain it to me. Calm down and explain it to me, Tad. Tell me. What is it that you wanted to know?"

"My grandmother," he huffed and explained, "was bi-racial. The slave master forced himself on my great-grandmother, and it always seemed like it was taboo to talk about it, you know. So I never asked my grandmother anything, but when you told me what happened to you, it just kinda brought it all back. How much my grandmother must have been carrying around because she was a result of something so ugly, so horrible, so terrible. How was her life? Was she ostracized for it? Payton, I found out that after my grandmother was born and they found out what she looked like, the slave master had her mom killed. His wife didn't want her, so my grandmother's grandmother raised her. I believe my grandmother blamed herself for her mother's death."

"You can't say that, Tad."

"I don't want to be angry at white people, but I am after finding all this out. I just don't know if I want to go to a major white university, running up and down a football field. I want a salary. The university gets paid off of black athletes, yet there are hardly any black coaches in the daggone NCAA. Like we're still their slaves. I don't know if I want to be a part of that. I'm sick that 170 or so years have passed and things are still the same."

"You know, I don't want you to think I don't understand. I understand, I feel you, and I was where you are not too long ago, if for different reasons. In my moment of racial anxiety, God allowed me to see that though it appears the same, it's not the same, Tad. It's not the same because we know Him, and His children can be different. God gives us grace every day, Tad, and out of that grace we have to forgive others."

I could see Tad was having trouble swallowing what I was saying. He walked a few steps away from me, shaking his head. However, I was determined to make his bitterness leave.

I continued talking behind him, "We have got to make this a better world; we've got to find a little peace of heaven here. I know there's a lot of things that aren't fair, but your grandmother wouldn't want you to give up, trade in your beliefs, and stop trusting God because of her life's experiences. She'd probably want you to trust Him even more. Love God even more, and give your white brother more love than you've ever done before. I had second thoughts about Georgia, but I know that I won't be alone up there. There'll be white people up there who think like me, you'll be there, and Christ will be in me, and He'll be in you. You miss your grandmother and that's OK. You'll see her again, but until then let's make her proud of how we live on earth. So, run for her at Georgia."

He hugged me tight. It was a hug of thanks, and I enjoyed it. I learned so much over the summer. I learned to forgive. I learned to reach out. And I learned to empathize with others. Those were good lessons I hoped never to forget.

In a nutshell, I was trying to let the Holy Spirit in me actually be the dominant figure so that I could think as Jesus thinks. I wanted to put others above myself because in that there's more joy than in personal accomplishments. In helping someone through a tough time, I found great fulfillment. Sometimes it's so easy in this life to not worry about anyone but yourself. The greatest reward and benefit, though, is when you invest in picking people up.

13

Saying Meaningful Good-Byes

Tad and I continued to embrace as the raindrops scarcely fell through a few leaves. Though the tree was protecting us well, we were starting to get damp. However, neither of us wanted to let go. *What's he thinking?* I wondered. I was concentrating so much on his thoughts that I didn't even realize what the embrace meant to me.

"Why does it seem so hard to say good-bye?" I asked him. "We're going to the same school and look at me. I'm getting teary-eyed."

"Yeah, we're going to the same school, but we got different agendas. It's the same place, but two different paths," Tad said with wisdom. "This embrace, for me, means a great deal because I don't know if our paths will cross at Georgia. Payton, I don't know if we'll be in the same circles. So many uncertainties."

"What, Tad?" I prodded. "It kinda seems like you wanna say something to me. What? You can tell me anything."

He looked away and then I placed my hand on the bottom of his chin and turned his cheek toward mine. My heart was beating fast with anticipation of his next word. The way he was, so timid, made me think whatever he was going to say wasn't going to please me, but I knew I needed to hear him.

"If you need me up there, call me. Though we're not an item, I still do love you." He reached up and placed an innocent kiss on my forehead. "Very much."

I just hugged him again. Couldn't bring myself to say I love you too, or let's cut the drama and be together again. I didn't know what to say, so I didn't say anything, but my hug was real. Whatever it meant, it was from the heart. It was serious. Maybe it was thank you. Yeah—a "thank you" for caring so much for me.

He pushed me, slightly, off him and broke our tight physical bond. I was kinda disappointed 'cause I didn't want it to end. However, reality set in and I knew it had to.

He made another sweet gesture when he said, "Let's pray. Let's pray for our time together at Georgia."

"That'd be great," I replied without hesitation.

Softly he held to my hand and led us, as he spoke in a voice of passion, "Heavenly Father, You're so awesome. It goes without saying how much we love You and thank You for allowing us to even go to college. Father, we just ask for protection as we journey on to a new place. That in our time there, although studying will be a priority, I pray we won't forget the first priority, and that's pleasing You. Come what may, I pray we'll grow not only academically but spiritually as well. In everything that we do, both individually and collectively, help us to do it with You in mind. I pray for the people we're going to interact with. Our teachers, even our parents, as they will have a sense of loss as they send us away. We pray for our friends back here, Father, that their lives will be great as well. I even ask a special prayer for Payton's friend, Lynzi, who's gone through some severe obstacles. Lord, I don't know where she is in her relationship with You, but I just pray You continue to knock on her heart's door. That in the midst of her pain, she may open it. Thank You again for sending Your Son Jesus to save our souls, Lord. May we be about Your business at Georgia. Thank You again for the opportunity to go there. In the name of Jesus we pray. Amen."

"Oooh, sounds to me like you and Tad just need to get back together," Dymond said as she, Rain, and I lay across my bed a week later.

We were having a sleepover. We had done it ever since we were about ten. Though I hated that Lynzi wasn't a part of our foursome this night, I was thankful I had Dymond and Rain over. We were getting kind of emotional. Not having them around was going to be tough, but hopefully our last night together would help. We could reminisce about things that happened years ago. And then when we get to college, we can look back on the closeness that we shared.

"No! No! No! We're just good friends. Hopefully we'll be able to be good friends at school. He just said some stuff that kinda shook me up. Like he didn't know what kind of person I was gonna be when I go to school, and that kinda bothers me."

"Why does that bother you?" Rain said.

"Because," Dymond cut in, reading my mind, or so she thought, "when this chick gets to school, after having 12:00 A.M. curfews and rules all her life and knows she won't have to answer to nobody, she might turn wild. Capital W-I-L-D. Poor, little sweet Tad wouldn't be able to take that."

"Ha, ha, ha," I joked back at her. "That's not even the case. I do have Somebody to answer to."

"Who? Your parents are gonna be right here in Augusta.

Like they gon' know what you doin'," Dymond expressed once again, thinking she knew everything.

"God can see all, Dy. He knows all. I have to answer to Him."

Neither of the two of them said a word. It's like that comment shocked them. Though it was going to be hard when I got to college not to step out there and try everything as Dymond suggested, in my mind the goal was not to stray from the Lord. Telling it to them helped me to believe that I could remain on the straight and narrow.

A couple of hours later, we were having even more serious girl talk. Rain and I were determined to ask Dymond why she and Fatz really broke up. They had been tight, and we knew Dymond still cared for him. Something had to have happened. Her explanation of irreconcilable differences just wasn't cutting it. There had to be more to it, and we wanted the dirt.

"Don't y'all look at me like that. I am not telling. I'm not talking about it. It's over. Done with. I'm pressin' on. I'm thinkin' about Howard and the Bison men and . . . that's where my mind is. I don't have time for no Fatz."

"What's up, girl? This is us. Go on. Let it out," I told her.

"Yeah," Rain let in. "We want to know. We tell you everything. C'mon, tell us."

Dymond couldn't even look at us. She got up and went to the window in my bedroom and then just flopped down beside it. She stared out the window as she told us a tale that even I couldn't believe.

"I still can't believe it myself. I mean I work at the drugstore. One day I was in there, this lady in her midtwenties, with the cutest little baby, came in. A baby boy. He was really sick, and I was ringing up the prescription medicine and stuff, and the baby wouldn't stop crying, and she was frustrated and everything. She needed some other medicine that wasn't behind the counter, and I couldn't find it, and the baby kept on crying. So anyway I came around the counter and asked her could I hold the baby, calm the baby down while she looked for the medicine. She just went on about how nice I was and we just started talking. It was late and nobody was really in the store. Plus, I was about to close. I ended up telling her what school I went to and then she said, wow, do you know this guy named Fatz. I said yeah, he's my boyfriend. She must not have heard me say he was mine because she said that he was the baby's daddy. She said he's my baby's daddy at the same time I was saying he's my boyfriend. She never heard me say he's my boyfriend, but I definitely heard her say he was my baby's daddy. So I figured out why his grades went down this year. He's had another life. Isn't that a trip? He's done a good job getting girls from the hood."

"She lives 'round there where you live?" Rain asked.

"Naw. Not my projects. The other side of town. Probably how we never found out about each other."

"Did you tell her you were Fatz's girlfriend?"

"I wanted to say something. I wanted to lash out. I wanted to hurt her, so that she would hurt Fatz, but I couldn't. I looked at that baby. He was so innocent. I didn't want to destroy his family, so I said nothing."

I pried, sure of the answer, "Fatz knows you know, right?"

"No. I told him I was movin' on, and to not ever call me again."

"And he's honored that?" I asked her.

"He tries calling, but I haven't let him know that I know or even talked to him long enough to break down and give in. I just kinda hang up right away and stay tough."

"You OK?" Rain came up to her and put her arm around her back.

Dymond quickly shook it off and said, "Yeah, I'm fine. No big deal. I'm fine."

Rain whined, "I wish I could take your toughness with me on to school. So that even with the uncertainty, I wouldn't have to worry about anything. I'd have on steel."

I knew that though Dymond said it and acted tough, the steel she wore and displayed for us wasn't as sturdy and strong as she let on. Even as she told the story with such emotion, I knew her heart was still breaking over this. Not only did Fatz have her heart, with her every day at school, but they had been physically intimate, and on many occasions. She had lost a special part of herself to a guy who was seeing someone else the whole time and she never knew it. Her trust in men was probably forever shattered. It just reminds me of another reason that Christ gives us the standard that can be the true shield to this kind of harm. That is staying pure 'til marriage. After hearing Dy's story, I was even more determined to follow His ways.

It was as if Dymond shook herself from the sadness that she felt inside because all of a sudden, she rose and headed straight over to Rain and said, "Well, what's up with you and Tyson? What's gonna happen when you go to school?"

"I wish I knew. I know that I'm gonna miss him like crazy, but he'll be at Georga Tech. At least we'll both be in Atlanta. I don't know. I'm trying not to think about it. We're gonna spend tomorrow together."

Changing the subject, I said, "I remember the time we almost got suspended for going along with everybody and almost stole those yearbooks back in middle school."

Rain and Dymond started laughing.

"Yep, good thing we didn't steal a yearbook too. Shoot, practically our whole seventh-grade class was out for three days."

"What was ever up with that? Why did people take 'em?" Rain asked. "They weren't that expensive."

I went on explaining, "Remember, we all said we didn't want one beforehand, and when the eighth- and sixth-graders came back with theirs, they looked so good we wanted one. Thankfully, we didn't want it bad enough to take one. Hindsight's 20/20 'cause I sure got a yearbook ever since then."

"And that's a good lesson to take to college," Rain said.

The three of us said together, "Buy the yearbooks."

We laughed and hugged most of the night. Then the tears started to flow. We couldn't hold our emotions any longer. We knew we'd miss each other greatly, yet there was nothing that we could do. We had to spread our wings and fly on our own. We could no longer be in the same nest, but leaving each other was not going to be easy, and it started to show. We were breaking down.

Still there was a missing link. However, we probably shared her tears, until there was a quiet knock on the door. I thought we were getting too loud with our emotions.

I yelled, "OK, Mom, we'll hold it down."

However, the door opened and there were more tears on the other side. It was Lynzi, standing there bawling in front of us. She immediately came up to me and hugged me tight.

"I'm so sorry," she whimpered. "I'm sorry. I'm sorry. If it wasn't for you calling the police or holding me together, I never . . . I never . . . who knows what would've happened? They never would've found me. I've been so mean and so mad that I couldn't even . . ."

Lynzi was having a hard time getting her words out. Though she wasn't making a lot of sense, I knew what she needed to say and wanted to say and was saying. So I stopped her.

"I understand," I said. "I know what you're feeling. You don't have to say you're sorry. I love you, girl, and even though I wasn't always the best friend I could be, my heart was always in the right place. I'll always care for the three of you guys. When I'm at Georgia and around new people, not knowing what's going on at Spelman, Howard, or in the army, I'll be prayin' that you guys are OK. I know that God will give me a sweet peace in my soul about that. I look forward to Christmas break when we can do another slumber party, but this time at somebody else's house before my mom and I get in trouble for real."

We'd gone through a box of tissues. My mom peered in the door and gave us another box. They all apologized to her for the vase that they broke around Debutante Ball time. My mom said that she wasn't excusing them, but she understood being young. She just hoped that we learned from what we'd been through this past year and not make those mistakes again.

We put on an old Boyz II Men tune, "It's So Hard to Say Good-Bye to Yesterday." As the song played, the memories of yesterday raced fast through our minds. I would hold on to them forever.

It was about three-fifteen in the morning, and we were asleep. I heard pebbles or something tapping on my window. It scared all of us. We were actually too frightened to move. Then we heard a familiar voice yelling.

"Please. Please. Please come out, Dymond. I need to see you," Fatz yelled. "Please come out."

"I'm not going out there," she said to us. "I have nothing to say to him. Don't open the window. Don't go to the door. He'll go away."

"Please come out," his cry got louder.

"Girl, I ain't tryin' to get in trouble for him. You got to say somethin' or I'm callin' the police," I told her very seriously.

My mom had to take me shopping to get things for my dorm room. The last thing I wanted was to hear sermons all the way to the mall and back. Dymond agreed to let up the window.

"Can we have a little private time?" Fatz yelled up the window.

"If you wanna talk to me, these are the terms. You have no negotiation power around here. It's over—don't you understand that? Over. I knew you were having to repeat the twelfth grade, but that's pretty simple for a kindergartner to comprehend. We're through. Leave."

"I know," he said "I know you found out. I spoke to Sadeka. She told me. She told me she met one of my classmates, and I put two and two together, but I need to explain."

"What in the world is there to explain, Fatz?" Rain interjected. "Another woman has your son. That kinda says it all."

"That's just like a brother, thinking he can have his cake and eat it too. Well, ain't no mo' dessert here, brotha. No more dessert here," Lynzi said.

We noticed Dymond, tough Dymond, start to shed more tears. This time it wasn't tears because she was sad to see us go. It was once again feeling overwhelmed with grief of the loss of their relationship. Lynzi and Rain pulled her back from the window. I talked to Fatz.

"Hey, guy, look. We were cool all through school, but for real, for real, it's time to grow up. You did my girl wrong, and I don't really have any respect for that and neither does she. We all make mistakes, but it's not like you guys can have a relationship, and she's not really ready to forgive you. You know that you could've told her before. You could've come clean. You have responsibilities that she doesn't want to be a part of. If you really do care like you say you care, cut the cord, man. Leave her alone. Let her go off to school remembering the good times. Don't rub it in her face why you betrayed what she thought you guys had."

"Will you just tell her I love her? Tell her the relationship with Sadeka just . . ."

"Yeah, whatever, Fatz! I'll tell her." I cut him off before he could lie.

Since he couldn't say anymore, I knew I needed to tell her so she could be strong and move on. He walked away and I let down the window.

I went over to her and said, "He told me to tell you that you were the best. He'll probably never have anyone as good as you and he knows that. He wants you to go and take care of your business up at Howard. Make us all proud like he knows you will, and that he won't be bothering you, but he wishes you the best."

"I thought he loved me," she looked into my eyes with despair and said, "And I was wrong. What happens when I get to school and I'm wrong again and I don't have you guys to turn to, or tell me to forget him, or have my back. Yeah, that's right. I need you guys to have my back. I'm tough, but I'm also human, and I love you guys too."

"I love you all too," Lynzi said. "I'll try this army thing out, and I know it's going to be tough, but I'll always be thinking about what college life is like. I got three great friends going to three great schools. I will know nothing about college."

"Oh, don't worry about it," I told her. "When you go, the army will pay for it."

We all laughed. Actually, we laughed until the next morning when they walked out of my house. They waved at me when they left. I waved back. Silently I asked God to go with them. Deep inside, I felt warm within as He gave me that peace I talked about, and let me know they'd be OK. They'd definitely be OK with Him in their lives.

"OK, Perry, whatever it is you wanna watch, that's fine," I said to him as I knew the romantic story I was watching on TV was not his type of show.

"Naw. Naw. Whatever you want to see. I'm cool. That's fine."

"Are you feeling OK?" I asked him.

"I'm cool. I'm OK."

"Why are you being nice to me? What do you want?"

"I don't know. You're leaving in a couple of days, and I don't wanna give you a hard time anymore. Is that OK? I want us to go out on a good note."

I went over to him and put him in a headlock.

"I wanna remember how we always are," I joked as we started wrestling.

After about five minutes of tumbling around he said, "Seriously, though, I'm going to miss you around here."

He didn't have much more to say, but the look on his face said much more than the words ever could. I too, would miss him terribly. I guess I never thought about it until right now. Maybe I didn't wanna think about it. All the people that I'd be forced to leave behind, as I head for my new world.

"Now you know anytime you wanna call me you can. Athens isn't that far away," I said to him, holding back the tears.

"I probably won't go to the University of Georgia, you know. After that, grad school. Getting a job. We might not ever be in the same city, much less the same house again. I mean, it's cool, but . . ."

"I know, it's sad."

"Yeah," Perry said as he held out his hand. "But it is a good sad."

I remember him following me around as if the only place to be was behind me. He kind of grew out of that in the last couple of years and started being my protector. I remember that fight with Dakari in the hallway the first day of my senior year. Though it was senseless, Perry was trying to defend my honor. I appreciated that in him. I now will not be able to look out for him as closely as I used to.

He had come into his own. Last year he ran the tenth grade. I'm sure he'd continue to be excellent in both academics as well as sports. His little girlfriend made the cheerleading squad. They'll be such a cute couple. Even if they don't make it as a couple to their senior year, I'm sure they'll be good friends.

Watch out for my brother, I said to the Lord silently as the two of us headed upstairs to the living room and dining room for dinner. *Watch out for him, please.*

"There's my grandbaby," my dad's mom said to me with open arms.

"Hey, Grandma!"

"Hey, baby!"

She had brought some of her sisters over, and my granddad was already sitting down at the table. My seventy-eight year-old granddad had so much spunk. Once we were all seated and the blessing had been said, we began digging in, enjoying the feast my mom had prepared. It was like Thanksgiving in August at the Skky home. No one was complaining, not even me, the guest of honor.

Pa Pa Skky said, "You know, God has truly blessed me. Not only am I feeling a little bit better than I was a few months ago, but I get to see my grandbaby get ready to go to college. I remember when you were born. I remember when you were dedicated. I remember goin' to dem dancin' ballet things recitals. You were so cute with them pigtails and curls. Yo' mama fix you up so nice. I remember saying, Lord, just let me see my little girl's next recital. I remember going to about, what, eight of them thangs. And each year you had on a different thing. Now I'm here to receive a big blessing. Not only did I get to see you graduate from high school, but I get to see ya go on out into the big world."

My mother was getting emotional and so were my grandmother and my great-aunts. My godmother was there also, and she was about to cry.

"Come here, child," Pa Pa said to me.

I got up and went over to him. He took my hand and placed it in his. His frail grip felt so secure.

"See all these folks around this table. They proud of you. You made us all proud. Now it's time to go make you proud. College is gon' groom you for who you gon' be. Saying good-bye is never easy, and just as I told the Lord all them years ago that I wanted to see another recital, I wanna share another meal with you. God's been good to me, and if I don't get to share that meal with you, I want you to know how much I love you. And that when I'm not here in body, look inside your soul and know that your ancestor and Christ lives inside of you, giving you the desire and power to do His will. Your dad and mom raised you with some good values. Now it's time you used that stuff, Payton, and don't stop 'til you get to the tip-top of the mountain. 'Cause when you stand there at the highest point in your life, all that it took to get there will be worth it. I know I'm at a high right now, holding hands with my grandbaby."

I bent down and hugged his neck. I loved my Pa Pa. I loved everybody at the table. And as I hugged him, the eldest of all I knew, it was giving me closure to the sadness I felt going to another place. Though it was tough thinking of life without them, I truly appreciated saying meaningful good-byes.

14

Dying for Peace

"Are you sure you'll be OK, baby?" my mom asked for the tenth time.

My mother, my father, and my brother drove me to college. They were all in the car about to drive back to Augusta. My mom held my hand extremely tight from the passenger's side window. Though she gripped me that way, I did not want her to let go. I knew that when she released the lock, I would have to step it up a notch.

The child in me would have to die. I would have to put away dependence upon my parents. Sure, they were paying part of my tuition, and my car insurance, health insurance, and so many other things. I mean, I was very blessed that my dad had set me up with a checking account before he left and a Visa card to go with it.

They had given me so many talks on what to do. What not to do. We prayed. We cried, but with the release of the grip, I'd have to get used to them not being there all the time. With my family not physically with me, I'd have to remember, and hopefully not stray, from their teaching. And though I really had wanted to be independent while in high school, now, with the release of my mom's beautiful manicured hand, I wouldn't have a choice but to be independent, and I was frightened. So much so, that my hand was shaking.

"Are you sure you'll be alright, baby?" Mother asked for the eleventh time as she felt my jitters.

A soft tear trickled from my face. And as if I was looking in the mirror, one dropped from hers at the same time. I leaned over and wiped her precious face. She wiped mine, and I kissed her on the jaw.

"I love you guys," I said to my dad, my mom, and my brother. "I'll be OK. You don't have to worry about me."

"All right now. That's enough good-byes. Payton, make us proud. We gots to go. Gots to get back on the road," my crazy daddy joked, trying to not let his emotions show.

I was his first good bullet, he always said. I knew he was gonna miss me, but having him be strong gave me the strength to let go of my mom's hand. I was a young adult. I had done it.

"Bye," I yelled out to them.

Watching that shiny, black Continental drive away left me feeling empty. That was a feeling that I didn't want to have. I just kinda stood there watching them until I couldn't see the car any longer. Inside, I heard myself scream for them to come back and get me. I was not ready to be grown. I still wanted to live with my mom and dad again. I didn't want responsibilities. High school was just fine.

"Come back. Come back. Come back," I moaned in a whisper.

They didn't come back. I had to go forward. Forward to my new home, a small dorm room, frail and old. Two beds, and a bathroom joining to another room on the side with two beds. My parents had gotten me there kinda early. Hardly anyone was there. And though there were three other young ladies that I would be connected to, I had met none of them yet. Being there early, I claimed my side. When you came into the room, passed the wooden door, my bed was the one across the room near the window. I sat on my bed and tried to be thankful for my blessings and not have a pity party.

I was thankful to my mom for taking the time to get me everything and more that I needed. I had a gorgeous straw trunk full of everything a college student could want, and a brand new laptop computer that my maternal grandparents gave me at the family dinner a few nights before. New make-up, new clothes, a fresh perm; I was hooked up. Ready to meet anybody, or so I thought.

Sitting on the brand-new maroon comforter set, I looked at the bed next to me and wished it were Rain's. I walked into the cold bathroom and peeped into the room on the other side and saw the two beds and so wanted them to be Lynzi's and Dymond's beds. However, I was brought back to reality when I heard the sound of the door in my room open. I quickly prayed.

"Father, please let me like this person, and let this person like me. I need a room that has harmony," I sighed. "Oh, I'm so nervous. Just make it work, Lord. Please."

"Hello, is anybody here?" a pleasant voice called out. "I don't know, Mother. I don't think anyone is here."

"Well look at the nicely decorated room. You have a roommate."

I assumed it was the girl's mother speaking. I couldn't just stand there and keep listening. I had to step out of the bathroom and step into their view.

"Hi. I'm Payton. That's my stuff," I waved after forcing myself to meet them.

I was making too much out of it, standing there wondering what they were thinking of me. My new roommate was white. That in itself was gonna be very different. Would she even wanna room with me? *Maybe I should ask her,* I thought. *What a foolish thought. Even if she doesn't want to, I'm not gonna leave, but that was foolish too. Help me, Lord.*

Deep inside I knew I was trippin', yet I couldn't help it. I was feeling it. Feeling the pressure of being different, and not knowing if that's OK. A gentleman came in carrying quite a few suitcases. Since I did not move from the bathroom doorway, the brunette-headed girl wearing a smiling face walked toward me.

She held out her hand and said, "Hi. I'm Laurel Casey Shadrach. I'm from Conyers, Georgia, and I'm your new roommate."

Wow, my grandparents were from there. But I didn't mention it then. I figured we could talk later and I could tell her.

"Hi Laurel," I extended my hand and replied. "I'm Payton. Payton Autumn Skky."

"It's nice to meet you Payton. Mom, this is Payton. Dad, this is Payton. Payton, these are my parents, Reverend and Mrs. Dave Shadrach."

"It's nice to meet you," I said as I shook her mother's hand.

"Payton. What a lovely name," Mrs. Shadrach said. "And you're from?"

"Augusta, Georgia, ma'am."

Her father put down the boxes and walked up to me with a stern voice and said, "Well, Payton from Augusta, Georgia, how lovely to meet you. Laurel, seems like you were blessed and got a pretty nice young lady for a roommate."

I was thinking in my mind, *Sir, you don't even know me. How can you say that I'm nice?* And though it was a silent thought, it was as if he heard me when he replied . . .

"I got a sweet peace about you, Payton. Yeah, Laurel, you're pretty blessed to have this lady as a roommate. I know you gals are gonna get along just fine."

"No, I want this bed," we heard an angry voice scream on the other side of the bathroom.

"Well, I want that one too," the other person yelled back.

"Should we go introduce ourselves to them?" I asked Laurel.

"Better let them calm down a second. If not, then maybe we'll go," Laurel wisely replied.

We had been talking for a few hours, just getting to know each other. Finding out our likes and dislikes. Not that we'd be able to know in the first sitting, but it'd be a good foundation and place to start.

Though we were different in color, we found out we were a lot alike. We were both from Georgia, we both had younger brothers—Laurel had three; I couldn't imagine Perry plus two more—and we both had ex-boyfriends going to Georgia. I already felt like we had a deep connection when she poured her heart out about her past relationship. Boy, could I empathize when she told me that a week before prom Branson Price broke up with her in the cafeteria, and she ended up going to the prom with her younger brother; though he was only one year younger, that in itself is pretty bad.

When she showed up at her prom, Branson was there with another cheerleader from her squad, Wendy Cartright, who she had thought was her best friend. What a terrible way to find out that she wasn't a friend at all. Though it was unfortunate that this Branson was going to Georgia, thankfully Wendy was at the University of Florida. Then I thought about it. *That's where my friend Jett goes to school.*

Out loud I said, "I'm gonna have to call Jett Phillips and tell him to watch out for this girl. Sounds like she'd get him into a whole lot of trouble. Way more trouble than he needs in his senior year."

"Did you say Jett Phillips? From the University of Florida? The . . . the . . . the quarterback? You're kidding right? You know him?" Laurel said in disbelief.

"Yeah, I know him. He's a friend of mine, and a pretty cool guy."

"I don't know about cool, but he is so cute."

Laurel was real, and I liked that. I could tell we were gonna be good friends. The same way that her dad felt about me, I now was sensing good vibes her.

"Well, you know my dad's a minister," she said. "And I don't want to alarm you, but I wanna pray. I'm a little apprehensive about being at Georgia. It's such a big school and I'm so far from home. Is saying a prayer OK with you?" she asked me.

I shook my head yes. My heart felt warm as I held her hand and we bowed our heads to pray.

"Do you wanna dial or hang up?" I asked.

"Oh my gosh! My friends and I say that too. Seems like it's been forever because we hadn't prayed together in a while, but we used to do that."

"I'll hang up," I told her.

"Cool," she said.

It was a different kinda cool. It wasn't the black "cooool" I was used to, but it was OK. We bowed our heads and she began.

"Most gracious heavenly Father, I come to You thanking You for all that You've done for me. You're so awesome. And as I was so unsure of whom I would have as a roommate, once again You've proven to be so faithful in giving me someone so much better than I could've ever asked for. Payton Skky seems so nice, so sweet, so humble, Lord. I just pray that as we begin to develop our friendship that You would be the center of it, Lord, and that we could honor You with our daily lives and enjoy our college experience.

We know it's going to be challenging, but we're Your children, and we can rest knowing You'll take care of us. Thank you."

She squeezed my hand and I continued to pray.

"Lord, I too share the same sentiments that Laurel expressed. You know how afraid I was. And being honest, Lord, afraid of rooming with a white girl. You've given me one that understands me, if not in full, at least in part, and has a heart to want to know who I am, and wants to respect me for who I am, and wants to be there for me, not because I'm anything but me. That's so awesome, or as she put it, that's so cool. I'm so thankful, Lord. I was so scared, Lord. I'm still somewhat afraid, but the faith Laurel talked about is real, right here, right now. You've proven that You're God by putting us together. And though we may sometimes let each other down, I pray that we'll be able to get through the rough times. And have more highs than lows, and that I'll be the type of friend that You call me to be, Lord, and that we'd be the type of students that make You proud. In Your precious Son Jesus' name, amen."

"Amen," she said.

"Aaaamen," a sarcastic voice said. "Yawl are praying. That's so cute."

We looked up at the petite blond-headed girl standing at the door. Both of us got up and went over to meet her.

"I'm Anna. I'm yawl's suitemate," the very country voice announced.

Before we could say anything, Anna was distracted by a noise she heard come from the other room. From our bathroom door to her side, she could see another girl placing things on the bed closest to the window.

Without even addressing her, she walked over to her and said, "No. You can't take this. I was just speaking . . . no. No. No," Anna started throwing the other girl's stuff on the floor. "I'm sorry, Jewels, but that's not fair. I went over trying to speak to our suitemates and now I find you trying to take that side. No, that's not gonna happen."

Jewels was so into picking up her things off the floor that she never even addressed us. Hearing the two of them was annoying and now I could tell why their noise was so loud from the other room, because hearing it firsthand was annoying.

"Hey, guys, I'm sick of all this screaming. I mean, there's gotta be a way to work it out," Laurel said to them.

The redhead stood up and said, "I'm Jewels Spivey, and I haven't had a chance to meet either of you, and to be quite frank, I think you two should handle what goes on that side of the bathroom," she pointed to our side of the room, "and not worry about what goes on over here."

"Well, if you two would talk to each other with some respect and not yell and scream so that we could hear in our side of the room, we wouldn't have to be in your business. The purpose of us coming over here was so that we could all get along. You know, kinda work it out together, since we are all sharing a bathroom," I suggested.

"Well, don't think I'm proud of that," this Jewels girl said in a smart tone.

I know she didn't just go there, I thought to myself. *This girl doesn't know me from a hole in the ground, but I'm gonna let that one slide and be the bigger woman, but if she says something out of the way one more time . . .*

"Though we are sharing the same room, doesn't mean we have to share the same space. When you're in there, I won't be. When I'm in there . . ."

"Yeah, I got it," I told her in a tone that shocked her. "Let me get out of your space right now."

I turned and walked to my room. I was getting angry. Luckily the telephone rang. I quickly jetted to the other side of the room and answered.

"Hello," thinking it was my parents. "I'm OK, Mom."

"Um, no, Payton. It's me, Tad. How you doin'?"

"Tad," I said as I sat down on the bed, happy to hear a friendly voice after going through the drama I'd just gone through with my roommates.

"I just got out of football practice and I had a little extra time before dinner. Is it OK if I stop by and see you real quick? Make sure things are going OK on your first day?"

"I'd love to see you!"

After I gave him directions, he said he'd be here in about thirty minutes. When I hung up the phone, Laurel saw the smile on my face.

"He's just a friend."

"Yeah, OK," she said sarcastically.

She and I both knew there was more to the grin that I had plastered from one ear to the other.

"Coming," I said when I heard the knock on the door about twenty minutes later.

"Are you Payton?" the friendly lady asked me.

"Yeah?"

"There's a gentleman outside waiting for you."

"Thanks," I told her and shut the door. "I'll be back, Laurel."

My room was on the bottom floor. Butterflies were flying around in my stomach as I walked from my room to the front desk. It had been a couple of weeks since I'd seen Tad, and I knew football had been very intense for him, and the last thing he needed was for our time together to be uptight. So I wanted to be in a good mood. Happy. Ready to welcome him with open arms.

However, to my surprise, I saw Dakari leaned up against the desk, flirting with a few girls in the hallway. My mouth fell to the floor. Surely he hadn't come to see me. So I turned around before he could catch a glimpse of my face.

"Nooo. Pay. Come here, babe. Come here. Let me talk to you. Don't go. Let me talk to you," he said, acting very strange.

Immediately I flew outside because I didn't want anyone in the foyer to hear what I had to say to him.

"What? What are you doing here? How did you even know I was staying here?"

"Forget all that. Forget all that. I just wanted to talk to you. I needed to talk to you."

"Forget nothin' . . . boy, you better tell me how you found me," I demanded.

"I called your brother. He gave me your new information. I had a couple of minutes before we go to the dining hall. I just wanted to come by on your first day and, um, you know, kinda straighten things out. I hadn't gotten a chance to talk to you in what, a couple of months. It's not like I don't owe you an apology. C'mon, let's hug and start off clean. Let's put everything behind us and start off clean. We're in college, you know—let's be cool."

Dakari started coming towards me. I quickly walked away from him and ran around the building. I unconsciously went towards the side where my dorm room was.

"Come here. Come here. Why are you trippin'?" Dakari asked me as if he couldn't understand why I wouldn't want to be in his embrace.

"I have nothing to say to you. Take your hands off of me!" I yelled at him as he tried once again to come too close.

Dakari grabbed my wrist. I wanted to get far away from him. Thankfully, I was saved. To my rescue came Tad Taylor.

"Payton, what's wrong?" he said, grabbing the guy from behind and throwing him to the ground. "What's up with you, man? Get off her. Can't you hear?"

Tad and Dakari were face-to-face. One not believing that it was the other. Though it was only a pause, it seemed like an eternity. In my mind I couldn't believe this was happening, didn't know what was gonna happen next, and was scared of what could possibly happen. And as if someone took off the pause button, they started going at it once more.

"Man, get off me! Who do you think you are? This is between me and Payton!" Dakari said to Tad.

"Between you and Payton? What you mean, between you and Payton? What? What? If she don't want you to touch her, then don't touch her! Can't you hear? Better step back, chump!"

I couldn't say, "Tad I'd handle this," because I didn't know if I could. The last time I was with Dakari I told him no, but he didn't stop right away. And even though we were right outside and we were on a college campus, I didn't know if he'd stop this time. And before he even began anything, I didn't want him to come too close. I was glad to be rescued by Tad's gesture of heroism.

What if Dakari was trying to be sincere? Trying to turn over a new leaf? Had Tad messed our ability to reconcile anything? I didn't know. All I knew was that they kept fussing and they kept tussling on the ground.

Dakari finally got ahold of Tad and grabbed him by the collar and threw him up against the dorm window. I was shocked to see three faces that I knew pressed against it. The only female faces I knew: Laurel, Anna, and Jewels.

They seemed to be beside themselves, and when Dakari tried to punch Tad, his hand went through he glass instead of Tad's face. Inside I was dying for the madness to end. I was dying of embarrassment. With all the problems and drama between Tad, Dakari, and myself, I was dying for peace.

15

Understanding What Counts

*T*he blood dripping profusely from Dakari's fist scared me, and I wasn't the only one. The three girls standing in my new dorm room were horrified as well. With the shattered glass came a big audience camped out around Tad, Dakari, and myself.

"Payton, what's going on?" Laurel screamed out the window to me.

"Y'all just step back. I got this. I got this," I said to them, stooping down as Dakari slumped under the window and cradled his hand.

"We need a towel," Tad said.

"Laurel, get me a towel out the bathroom. Please. Please. I have some towels right there. They're maroon," I yelled.

She threw one out the window. As Tad tried to wrap it around Dakari's badly damaged hand, Dakari once again attacked in anger, not wanting help. Before the two of them could get into it again, campus police came. The two uniformed officers broke through the crowd and immediately took Dakari and Tad away.

I was in tears. Though it wasn't my fault, I felt it was. Somehow I felt responsible. Though I couldn't control what had happened, I felt worried about what was to come. I ran back inside, grabbed my car keys and my purse, and tried desperately to find the campus police station.

After going around in a big circle twice, I got so frustrated. I wanted to help and I was unable to. After being disappointed with not being able to find the place, I just pulled in the parking lot with tears continuing to flow so heavy that I felt weak. I was weak on the inside and sad on the outside. I guess I was just tired of having it all bottled up inside. Boyfriend issues, new place issues, race issues. There were too many issues for one person to deal with. A person can only take so much before finally coming to a point of breaking.

"Father, help me make sense of all this stuff swimming around in my head. It's making me wanna drown, and I need You to help me. I need to be clear on a lot of this stuff and I'm not, Lord. All I know is there is much confusion, and You are not a God of confusion. A stronghold is what I need. Help me, Lord. Help me," I cried as I looked above.

After I wiped my eyes and asked a few students walking, I was finally directed to the campus police station. Without hesitation, I walked in and asked about Tad and Dakari. The secretary told me that they weren't brought there. They were taken to the football coach's office and that I probably didn't have to worry.

I guess I felt somewhat better as I walked out of the building. *At least they aren't in jail,* I told myself, *but they could get kicked off the team and lose their scholarships. Maybe Dakari will be okay. His parents can pay for him to go to school, but Tad. Tad will have to drop out. This is horrible.*

Finally I pulled up in front of the football dorm. I just stared at it. There was no way I could go in. Like the head football coach would want to talk to me. That would be a no! I'm the one that caused this mess between the two of them. So I just went back to my dorm room and realized that I could not fix everything.

When I got back to my room Laurel wasn't there. The glass was picked up and cellophane was covering the window. Because I was dejected, I wasn't making a sound. I was just in a daze, wanting this nightmare of a situation to be a myth instead of my truth.

The voices on the other side of the room through the bath got loud. I was fed up. I couldn't take any more arguing. I was about to go over and let Jewels and Anna have it. When I stood up and stepped into the bathroom, I was caged by what I heard.

The voice of Jewels said, "Well, I'm trying to get into a sorority, and having a black roommate will not help my cause."

"Well, I wanna pledge too, and I don't know if Jewels is totally right, but I share her concerns," Anna agreed.

"Of course I'm right," Jewels cut in and said. "Plus, it's not just the fact that she's black, but look at the kinda people she hangs out with. They were fighting like animals."

"What's that saying," Anna replied, "you can take people out of the ghetto, but you can't take the ghetto out of people. I don't wanna bring the ghetto in my room. Maybe you should start looking for a new roommate too. I mean, your reputation could be damaged. Why would you even want to room with her? She can't understand who we are."

What is going on? I thought to myself. *They don't even want to room with me anymore. Is it because I'm black or is it because my friends are crazy? I don't know, gosh, I have a headache. I just don't know, but Laurel doesn't deserve this. Maybe I should just tell her I don't wanna room with her either.*

151

Before I could possibly say that, I heard Laurel say, "Well, you know what, guys? She may be black, that's true, and she may be going through some serious stuff; that's obvious with what we just witnessed today. I don't know her well, but I think I know her a little bit better than I know the two of you. Let me ask you a question. Are either of you guys Christians?"

"Well, I'm Catholic," Anna said.

Jewels interjected, "No, I'm not a Christian. What does that have to do with anything? We're talking about getting into a sorority, not getting into heaven. That Payton girl is going to ruin all of our chances. Being a Christian isn't going to help anything right now, but maybe telling her in a nice way to get out. If *you* can't tell her nicely, then *I'll* just have to tell her to move out."

Jewels walked to the other side of the room. She and Anna were very upset. At that point, so was I.

"Well, let me just say this. Her skin color doesn't matter to me. I too want to pledge. My mom was an Alpha Gamma, and it's my first choice, but if it doesn't work out, it's OK. Contrary to what you guys think, being a Christian is the most important thing, and I'd rather be her roommate over you two any day. Because with God on our side anything is possible, but when stuff gets in the way and all we care about is what we want, nothing can happen. Sometimes disaster happens. Payton needs a friend right now, and if you guys aren't up for it, that's fine, but I am. And don't tell me what's good for me because you don't know the same God I know, and unless you are tapped into what He wants for me, you could never tell me what I need."

My back had turned to the bathroom door. Laurel tried to open the door, but couldn't because I was blocking it. She pushed and pushed, and then I finally realized she was trying to get through. So I stood up and let her in. She flipped on the light and saw my anguish.

Wiping my tears, she said, " It's OK."

"No, it's not OK. They don't even like me. I miss my family. My friends, they are in a lot of trouble. I'm just not OK right now."

"Did you hear what I told them?"

I nodded my head yes.

"Payton, you do know the God that I know, and because you know Him, it's OK. He can give you the strength to face stuff that's tough. It wasn't easy telling those girls over there that I didn't care what they thought. A couple of years ago, I wouldn't have been able to say that. Back then, I didn't let the power inside of me work, but it's working now, and I'm stronger. Still struggling in some areas. Believe me, I got problems, but when I tap into the Holy Spirit and let that light shine, I amaze myself sometimes, and I'm pretty proud right now. Jewels and Anna, I'm not going to give up on them. They have something wrong with them in the way they perceive stuff, but they need to know God too. Until they do, we need to stick together 'cause we do know Him, and we need to encourage one another 'cause I'm sure there's going to be a time when I'm going to need you," Laurel shared with the utmost concern.

We gave each other a big hug and walked into our room. I was thankful she cared so deeply. Her words eased my aching heart.

It was hard sleeping that night because I couldn't stop thinking about the day's events. Though Laurel had given me so much encouragement, and we had gone out to eat and had a good time laughing, reality surrounded me, and reality was pretty gloomy.

My suitemates were in favor of my presence there to end. Dakari and Tad . . . well, at that point who knew what was going on with them? Slumber, restless slumber, was not an option. Finally, the phone rang, and I jumped at it. I was hoping it was Tad or Dakari. It was my mom.

"I couldn't sleep, pumpkin. I was just thinking about you," she said.

"Mom, what are you doing up so late? It's eleven."

"I know. I just couldn't get thoughts of you off my mind. The first day at school, how was it?"

I couldn't tell her about everything that happened. I didn't want her to worry more. I was worrying enough for both of us.

"I'm still here, but I miss you," I said to her.

"That makes your mom feel real good. I miss you too. My baby girl is on her own. I'm proud of you. Have you had a chance to unpack everything?"

"No. The day was a little overwhelming."

"Well, I put a bag in your closet, and it has a present in it. If you find yourself like me, unable to sleep, maybe you could go over and peek at it. You know I'm praying for you."

"Yes, ma'am," I said. "I just wanna make you proud, and I don't know if I can do that."

"Just remember," my mom said in the sweetest tone, "I am proud of you, and so is your dad. We love you unconditionally, baby. Do what you have to do for you, and always know we're here. Good night."

"Good night, Mom."

I needed to hear that. I needed to know that my parents were in my corner. I was so thankful to the Lord for allowing her to call at that time, but I still needed to hear from . . .

Before I could finish that thought, the phone rang again. I quickly picked it up because I didn't want to wake Laurel.

"Hello," I mumbled in quite a sad tone.

"Payton, heeey. It's me," Tad voiced.

"Hey, guy. I've been waiting to hear from you."

154

"You OK?" he asked.

"Physically, yeah. I mean, my heart is beating a little fast. Every time I think of what happened . . ."

"I'm sorry about that," he cut in and said. "It got a little out of hand. I don't know. When I heard Dakari say he tried to force himself on you, and he was possibly trying to invade some more of your space, it just got me a little crazy, ya know. I shouldn't have reacted that way."

"Well, you sound pretty calm. Tell me. What's been going on with you guys? I mean what happened?"

"Well, Coach called us into his office and basically went off on the two of us. Called us some of everything, and the running back coach was in there too. He was also pretty hard on us. Dakari had to see the trainer. His hand's gonna be all right though. It wasn't as bad a cut as we thought, but he did have to get a stitch."

"A stitch," I joked.

"One stitch," Tad said. "But, um, they were gonna kick us off the team and take away our scholarships."

"Well, obviously they didn't. Didn't you say they weren't? Tell me what happened."

"Well, Coach asked what did we wanna do. He said he didn't want this type of fighting going on with his teammates. Said he wanted people to be close. So he said either we can leave this program, or we can elect to race."

"Race? What do you mean?"

"Up and down the stadium. First one that does it fifty times is a winner and gets to pick which bed he wants in our room. Coach made us room together. Can you believe that? The winner gets to pick the daggone bed. Top bunk or bottom bunk."

I kinda giggled along with Tad. Seeing the two of them as roommates was very hard to imagine. Those arrangements seemed worse than mine. I couldn't believe a race saved their positions on the team.

"After we moved into our room together, we just kinda been talking all day. We ain't tight, but I figure maybe God wants me to minister to your boy."

"Wow," I cut in, "that's deep, Tad. Dakari needs spiritual direction too."

"Also, I just want to apologize to you for coming over there and jumping into something that really didn't need to happen. I just kinda made it worse. I should have talked to my roommate. I know Dakari broke a window in somebody's room. Coach said the football department would pay for it, but I feel responsible and I'm sorry. I'm sorry for embarrassing you and . . . I'm just sorry for my part in it," Tad expressed with sincerity.

"Well, that was actually my dorm room window," I cut in and said. "They are supposed to fix it tomorrow, my roommate told me. Don't worry about it. I'm just glad you two guys are OK. I'm glad that it's working out."

"We are unable to go off the premises, you know, the football area, for a week. So I won't get to talk to you, plus the football season is about to start. I'll be calling you every now and then to let you know I'm thinking about you. So is my new roommate, who also wants to say hello. Is that OK?"

"Yeah. See ya, Tad. Take care," I said.

"Hey, Pay," Dakari said.

"So, I hear you got a new roommate?" I teased.

"Yeah. Yo' boy is all right. We ain't got no choice. Um, look here, Payton. Earlier, I just wanted to tell you I'm sorry, and now I am ending up telling you again. I care about you, and I just keep going about telling you the wrong way. Trying to show you how much I care. Um, I need you to forgive me. I just need to hear you say you forgive me. Well, maybe now, it's too much to ask?"

"It's not too much to ask, Dakari. You just scare me sometimes. I don't know what you're thinking. I don't know how to read you. I used to know you so well."

"To be honest with you, I'm kinda glad yo' boy did come along. I was trying to grab you and pull you close to me and stuff. Just gotta learn to control myself. Not that I was gonna do anything to you or nothin' like that. I think that was a little extreme, but I understand you didn't know."

"Dakari, I forgive you. We can use some grace. You love God, right?" I said to him.

"Yeah. Yeah, I think I do. I don't always show it, but . . ."

"Well, the same grace He's given me, I'm giving you."

"Well, lady, we'll talk to you soon. Don't worry about us. We won't tear each other up in here."

I hung up the phone with the two of them with a smile on my face. That was going to be interesting. Hmmm, the two of them roommates.

"Wow," I said out loud.

The phone rang once more that evening.

"Who could that be at this hour?" I said.

"Hey girl!" Lynzi yelled.

"It's me! It's me!" Dymond said.

"And it's me!" Rain said.

"Hey, y'all!" I turned over in my bed and replied. "What is going on?"

"I'm still here," Lynzi said. "I haven't left yet, so I called your parents and they gave me the new number, and we just wanted to say hey. So how's things been going up there in Athens?"

"I miss y'all. That's for sure."

We talked for about thirty minutes, and they caught me up on what had been going on with each of them. After they heard my story, they all joked they were transferring and coming to the University of Georgia because there was too much drama up here to miss.

As I talked, I knew I'd miss my friends, but hearing them say they would miss me too meant a lot. Certain things in life were too small to even worry about. I had to stop stressin', or it was going to take me to a point where I didn't want to be. Restless nights weren't good for me. College students need to be prepared for every day.

Before going to bed, I went over to the closet and looked at the bag my mother told me about. There was a present beautifully wrapped in gold. Laurel hadn't awakened through all of my conversations and all my loud talking; I didn't want to disturb her now with all my fiddling around.

There was a little card inside that said, "Make every day count. The world is yours. Enjoy the college experience, and keep a journal of your precious memories. One day maybe we'll share them. Love, Mom."

I turned on the light next to me. I knew I needed to say my prayers, but I thought I'd do something different. Instead of saying a prayer, I'd actually write down what I was feeling. I began to write:

Father in Heaven,

You know the things I struggle with. And You're always right there to see me through. I think I finally got ahold of this color issue that's been weighing me down. Sometimes not being happy with who I am because that was not the cool thing to be. And not liking people that are different from me just because they were different. Or being on edge in certain situations—unsure of the outcome. You know—like going to a major white university and being black. And being afraid that I won't fit in.

You know, Lord, along the way though, You've given me people that showed me some of that hatred that I didn't even realize was bottled up inside didn't need to be there. Everybody is not the same, and race, though it's a tough issue, can be conquered when put into its proper perspective. Neither black nor white is better. I'm thankful for my aunt, who told me that she dreams of a world that will one day be filled with people who all have a heart for You. And letting me run into a young white guy who's got it going on, and will stop and take time to say, "Hi," and be himself and like me because of me. And let me see that we can share common interests and be friends. Or giving me a roommate who, though different, isn't that different at all. And will stay by my side when people tell her she shouldn't.

Through those people, I learned what's important. And that is having the blood of Jesus flowing through my soul. In the end, that's all that's going to matter. Being white or black won't make a difference. Just like the physical race saved Tad and Dakari from being off the football team, being a member of the Christian race will save a person from eternal separation from You. I thank you, Lord, that I'm saved because, above all, that's what's important. I am so grateful that as a freshman in college I'm finally understanding what counts.